GARDENER T[...]

FRÉDÉRIC RICHAUD was born [...] teacher and journalist. *Gardener to the King* is his first novel.

BARBARA BRAY, formerly Script Editor of Radio Drama at the BBC, has twice won the Scott-Moncrieff Prize, as well as the French-American Foundation Prize, for her translations.

"A gem of a novel steeped in the discreet seduction of this world of trees and fruits . . . Based on a rigorous historical documentation and on a fascinating compromise between the factual and the imagined"   **MARTA MORAZZONI,** *Corriere della Sera*

"Frédéric Richaud's wonderful first novel is as splendid and sordid as the Sun King's court: beautifully constructed but full of ugly things . . . whether describing a masked ball, Lucullan banquet or the advent of Halley's comet, Richaud makes the reader share in the participants' fear and excitement. He is a concise and witty writer"   **MARK SANDERSON,** *Time Out*

"The freshest and most original of novels"
GIUSEPPE CONTI, *Giornale*

"This delicately crafted little allegory evokes memories of both Voltaire's *Candide* and José Saramago's teasing parabolic fiction . . . It's a beautiful piece of work"   *Kirkus Reviews*

"An intensely poetic sap emanates from this first novel with its vivid yet carefully controlled style. Flavours, colours and smells blend in this garden in full bloom, in which the tragic sense of life comes to maturity"   *Nouvel Observateur*

"In this adroit translation by Barbara Bray, Richaud paints a vivid picture of the inequities of prerevolutionary France"
HELEN PITT, *New York Times*

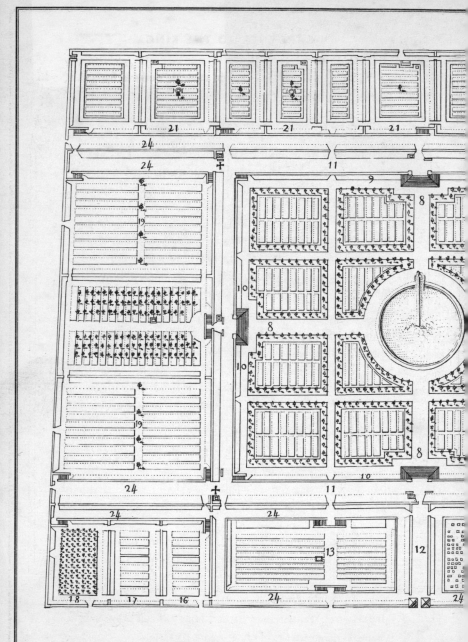

PLAN OF THE KING'S VEGETABLE

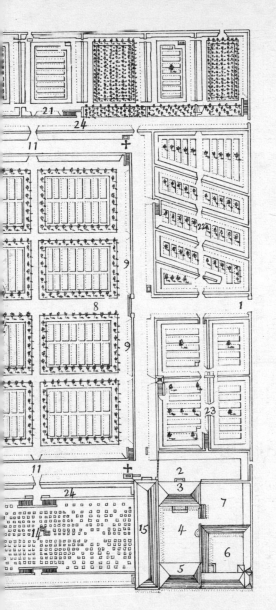

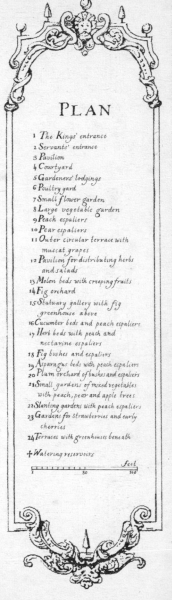

PLAN

1 The Kings' entrance
2 Servants' entrance
3 Pavilion
4 Courtyard
5 Gardeners' lodgings
6 Poultry yard
7 Small flower garden
8 Large vegetable garden
9 Peach espaliers
10 Pear espaliers
11 Outer circular terrace with
   muscat grapes
12 Pavilion for distributing herbs
   and salads
13 Melon beds with creeping fruits
14 Fig orchard
15 Statuary gallery with fig
   greenhouse above
16 Cucumber beds and peach espaliers
17 Herb beds with peach and
   nectarine espaliers
18 Fig bushes and espaliers
19 Asparagus beds with peach espaliers
20 Plum orchard of bushes and espaliers
21 Small gardens of mixed vegetables
   with peach, pear and apple trees
22 Slanting gardens with peach espaliers
23 Gardens for strawberries and early
   cherries
24 Terraces with greenhouses beneath

✝ Watering reservoirs

Feet

GARDEN AT VERSAILLES

Frédéric Richaud

GARDENER
TO THE KING

Translated from the French by
Barbara Bray

THE HARVILL PRESS
LONDON

First published with the title *Monsieur le jardinier* by Bernard Grasset, Paris, 1999

First published in Great Britain by The Harvill Press in 2000

This paperback edition first published in Great Britain in 2001 by
The Harvill Press, 2 Aztec Row, Berners Road, London N1 0PW

1 3 5 7 9 8 6 4 2

www.harvill.com

© Éditions Grasset & Fasquelle, 1999
English translation © Barbara Bray, 2000

This book is supported by the French Ministry for Foreign Affairs, as part of the Burgess programme
headed for the French Embassy in London by the Institut Français du Royaume-Uni

i institut français

Frédéric Richaud asserts the moral right to be identified as the author of this work

A CIP catalogue record for this book is available from the British Library

ISBN 1 86046 877 2

Designed and typeset in Fournier at
Libanus Press, Marlborough, Wiltshire

Printed and bound in Great Britain by Mackays of Chatham

Plan of the King's Vegetable Garden at Versailles (ppii–iii) by Emily Hare

The illustrations that appear throughout are reproduced from a facsimile edition of Jean-Baptiste de La
Quintinie's *Instructions pour les Jardins, Fruitiers et Potagers* (1690) published by Actes Sud, Arles in 1999

For Jean-Philippe

I

August 1674. At Versailles all the talk was of war. After the King's dazzling victory over Holland and what was seen as its overweening ambition, his two best generals, though formerly enemies, now joined forces to halt the European coalition that had just burst through France's northern borders. At Seneffe in Belgium the once-rebellious Prince de Condé was holding back the onslaughts of William of Orange. The flaring up of the campaign in the Low Countries filled the air with the clamour of drums, artillery and the cries of men. Each side counted its dead in thousands.

On the frontier with Lorraine the peasants of the Palatinate had been and still were ruthlessly slaughtering anyone representing the authority of the King. Terrifying accounts filtered through to Versailles of how on moonless nights rustics armed with pitchforks and knives as long as a man's arm would appear out of the darkness, slit the throats of French soldiers, then vanish among the trees only to materialise again the next day somewhere else — it might be anywhere. But by the grace of God, Turenne, the saviour of Alsace, had introduced a policy of such brutal repression that it was hoped he would soon quell these fearsome yokels. Villages were being torched, whole communities massacred.

Day after day the gardens and galleries of Versailles seemed to echo with the din of battle or with the fainter but perhaps more terrible sound of flints whetting German blades. For twenty-four hours distraction might be provided and fear allayed by some magnificent court entertainment, the beauty of Athénaïs de Rochechouart, the tinkling of fountains or the music of the divine Lully. But next day everyone would be anxious again: was the army still advancing, how many prisoners had been taken, how many standards captured from the enemy? Usually the reports issued daily by the King and Colbert were tantalisingly terse: "The court may rest assured that Condé and Turenne are on the verge of victory." Naturally the court wanted to know more, and people spent hours watching out for the arrival of weary emissaries bearing accounts of their masters' manoeuvres. But the messengers were incorruptible and it was impossible to find out what was really going on.

Condé and Turenne came to seem like heroes of myth. It was said of Condé in particular that after three horses had died under him one day in battle against the Dutch, he had called for a fourth and charged on alone in pursuit of the fleeing enemy.

When they weren't shaking with fear at the thought of seeing a foe rise up before them in a dark alleyway or at a turn in a corridor, some courtiers had visions of becoming modern Alexanders themselves and performing great deeds of self-sacrifice or revenge. They never tired of telling admiring ladies how they would set out at once for the blood-soaked battlefields if only urgent matters didn't oblige them to remain in attendance on the King.

→>-<-

Jean-Baptiste de La Quintinie was unconcerned by such agitations. He lent only half an ear to the gory tales people told him, and observed from a distance the growing unease at court and the messengers' ceaseless comings and goings. It wasn't that he took no interest in the progress of the war and the fate of its heroes. He knew Condé well and was glad to hear of the exploits that were bringing him fresh glory. But he had a war of his own to fight, a war that was long and silent, a war that nobody talked about.

La Quintinie's own grand manoeuvres had begun four years ago, after the King had relieved him of his duties to Fouquet and made him Steward of the Orchards and Kitchen Gardens of Versailles. The King's instructions had been quite clear. One day as he and his entourage were strolling along the paths designed by Le Nôtre, the monarch suddenly turned to his new gardener and said:

"Do you know what I expect from the artists who work for me, Monsieur de La Quintinie?"

"No, Sire."

"Perfection, monsieur – perfection. And, Monsieur de La Quintinie, you are an artist."

And that demand, those expectations, far from annoying La Quintinie, had won him over.

The three hectares for which he was responsible, and which, in the days before the great château was built, had supplied enough provisions for king and court after hunting parties and other country pleasures, had more recently had to be enlarged and redesigned to cope with heavier and more exacting requirements. Louis and his guests had taken to visiting Versailles more and more often once spring had arrived. So La Quintinie had improved the overall quality of the soil by the addition of clay, silica and chalk, and treated most of the beds with lime. He had new drains dug, and oversaw his men as they sowed seeds, built greenhouses and planted fruit trees.

Once the new soil started to bring forth its first products, ranging from the most familiar to the rarest of varieties, the struggle became more subtle but perhaps even more arduous — exhausting in summer when there was too little rain, and uncomfortable in autumn when there was too much, while in winter there was frost to be guarded against. All the year round the garden was threatened by predators — birds, mammals and insects. So the gardener had his own campaigns, his own devoted army, his own weapons of wood and steel, his own victories and defeats.

→><

From the day he was appointed, La Quintinie was an object of curiosity. Little was known about him save that the King had taken a fancy to him and that some years ago he had abandoned the law and taken up horticulture. But why had he cut short what according to those who knew him then was set to be a brilliant career? Had he been influenced by a visit to the botanical gardens at Montpellier? Or by his travels in Tuscany and the country around Rome? No one knew. But wherever it was that fate dictated a new turning, everyone believed God must have been behind the revelation, so much pleasure did his work bring to the souls as well as the bodies of those who enjoyed its results.

At one period he had worked for Fouquet at Vaux-le-Vicomte, together with the architect Le Vau, the gardener Le Nôtre and the painter Lebrun, the three other magicians now working together to create the splendour that was to be Versailles. No one had forgotten Fouquet's sudden fall from grace: the former minister of finance, now imprisoned for the rest of his life for embezzlement, had really been brought low because his ostentatious life-style had aroused the wrath and envy of the King. But for fear of reawakening Louis' ire, people never referred to all that.

⇥⟩⟨⇤

Though most of the courtiers liked or even admired La Quintinie, some were jealous of the way the King went to visit him among his plants, sometimes spending hours watching him at work in a trench or up a tree. The gardener seemed oblivious of the royal presence.

Some said he was a Protestant, others that he was a former rebel and an avid reader of La Rochefoucauld's *Memoirs*. Others again accused him of atheism, alleging that they had heard him praising Vanini and his *Admirandis Naturae*. Once it was even rumoured that the letters he exchanged with eminent English and Italian botanists embraced matters other than seeds and technical discussions about how to grow radishes. The King, under pressure from those about him, once ordered Bontemps, his head valet, together with his blue-uniformed men, to spy on the gardener's doings for a few weeks. But they observed nothing out of the ordinary.

⇥⟩⟨⇤

La Quintinie sometimes worked in his garden for days on end without putting in an appearance at court. And when his detractors did catch sight of him in one of the palace corridors they would take the opportunity to mock his lack of elegance. His rapid gait contrasted oddly with the awkwardness of his gestures. "He ought to engage the services of a dancing master." He went bareheaded and wore working clothes, with breeches, stockings and shoes all spattered with mud. "A tailor wouldn't come amiss, either." In the presence of those in high places he said little: you could tell he was only waiting for the moment when he

[5]

could escape once more to his own domain. "Not to mention a tutor of rhetoric."

But as soon as he was in his kitchen garden again his pace grew more relaxed, his movements graceful and precise. He knew every plant and insect by name. In the evening, as the shadows lengthened, people would come to talk to him, to profit not only from his knowledge of fruit and vegetables and the seasons, but also from the simple wisdom he had learned from the world over which he ruled.

→>-<←

La Quintinie seldom joined in the lavish festivities the King continued, war or no war, to provide. Dazzling displays of horsemanship clearly bored the gardener. So did the tournaments in which Monsieur, the King's eldest brother, showed off his skill with the lance. La Quintinie often turned up, full of apologies, after the proceedings had begun, or sometimes when they were over. Occasionally he vanished just as Monsieur was about to make a particularly impressive charge.

"No doubt Monsieur de La Quintinie has something better to do."

"His work *is* very demanding . . . "

"Don't you think, Monsieur de Courtois, that I too would like to slip away whenever I felt like it from a tedious walk or an expensive game of cards?"

"Why don't you, then, my dear fellow?"

"Surely you know the rules? I know what would happen to *me* if I blithely abandoned *my* post. Have you forgotten what happened to the Comte de Rey a few months ago?"

"I know nothing of it. What did happen?"

"He made it a point of honour to appear at court as rarely as possible. He said he preferred his beloved countryside near Rouen. Then one day he needed to present a request to the King. And do you know what the King said to the official in charge of arranging audiences? 'Monsieur le Comte de Rey?' he asked, when the list of petitioners was read to him. 'Never heard of him.' The story spread like wildfire, and everybody said they'd never heard of him either. So now he can enjoy his famous countryside to his heart's content. He hasn't a friend in the world."

+>-<+

La Quintinie was not married, and as far as anyone knew he had no women friends. Some people attributed this to his unduly prolonged studies and his devouring passion for horticulture, which left him no time for falling in love.

Yet over tea the Marquise de Cabannes would tell any lady who cared to listen how years ago a rich young widow, Madame de Rouque by name, had fallen madly in love with him. For months she pursued him, imploring him to return her passion, but the gardener, completely bound up in his work, remained unmoved. Madame de Rouque died of a broken heart. If La Quintinie now shut himself up in his garden, as another man might withdraw to a monastery, it must be because he was affected more deeply by her death than he had ever been prepared to admit.

True or false, this doleful tale intrigued some women, and every so often a few of them would go and gaze at La Quintinie toiling alone in his garden, bearing in silence the burden of an ancient sin.

+>-<+

La Quintinie paid no heed to such comments about him as came

[7]

to his ears, whether the gossip was due to jealousy or to admiration. All he cared about was his fruit and vegetables, and the weeds and insects that were a permanent threat to them. He was driven body and soul by the desire to provide for the King and his guests. Small and inactive though he might be in comparison with the generals promoting the glory of France far away, he had resolved to contribute to the glory of his King here before all the world.

+>-<+

A few weeks earlier the gardener had mingled with the crowd of peasants and seasonal workers who had gathered to watch the arrival of the court at Versailles. Though the sight was familiar by now it never ceased to fascinate him. The King's red coach, tossing up clouds of dust, drawn by six white horses and flanked by musketeers, drove into the great Cour de Marbre, the marble courtyard overlooked by the royal apartments. The King's coach was followed by a long line of carriages and an even longer procession of wagons and carts laden with cupboards, chandeliers, tables and marble busts. Slowly the crowd of travellers dispersed into the apartments and corridors of the château or disappeared along the garden paths.

At all hours of the day and sometimes even at night the palace was invaded by petitioners, tradesmen, workmen, flunkeys and an ever-growing number of prostitutes. Soon, despite daily cleaning, the gilt and stucco ornamenting the apartments and the grand staircases became impregnated with the smell of excrement.

But noise and odours alike, floating from the windows, faded away before they reached the kitchen garden.

+>-<+

It was harassing work, running the garden. Every morning for more than a month men had been going in and out of its various enclosures humping baskets of apples or oranges on their backs or carrying hurdles and stretchers laden with grapes, figs and pears. Wheelbarrows were needed to transport pumpkins and cabbages. But La Quintinie never wearied of supervising such work, though it might take several hours, depending on the size of the order. He examined all the boxes and baskets one by one, removing all imperfect specimens, which were sent to the royal stables or pheasantry. He neither knew nor cared what happened to his produce once it left his garden. If anyone asked the reason for this indifference he would shrug and say, "My fruit and vegetables go to feed humanity." The pride and pleasure he took in this simple certainty were enough for him.

In the evening, after the workmen had gone home, he often stayed on by himself, writing or sketching in one of the little notebooks he kept in his pocket. The garden needed to be made to yield much more. He would roam tirelessly back and forth along the box-lined paths, dreaming up new layouts, different crops, all kinds of improvements. It was usually late at night before he returned to his apartments.

People jested that one day his feet would sink into the earth, leaves and moss would sprout from his ears, and his arms would turn into branches.

→>-<←

Towards the end of the summer, when news of Turenne's and the Grand Condé's victories was confirmed, the atmosphere grew calmer. Though conversation in the corridors or out in the gardens still turned occasionally on stories of battles, most talk was now concerned with the King's latest love affair.

"His head's been turned by Scarron's widow!"

"Who?"

"Scarron's widow – governess to Madame de Montespan's children."

"Who told you that?"

"No one. I just know."

Then suddenly, at the beginning of October, corridors, gardens and fountains all fell silent. The court had followed the King to Paris, where the accommodation was more comfortable at this time of year.

II

Not many stayed behind at Versailles; a few lackeys kept on for the winter, a handful of guards with nothing to do, a score of workers building the grand Staircase of the Ambassadors under the direction of François Dorbay. Now it was to the pounding of hammers and the grating of saws that the corridors echoed, though occasionally through the men's guffaws and whistles crept memories of Lully's gentle harmonies, of the rustle of fountains and the soft exclamations of women.

La Quintinie was happy living in a deserted Versailles. His work wasn't brought to an end by the migration of the court. He still had to maintain a mild and regular temperature in the asparagus beds and among the rows of cabbages and carrots. He still had to plant the tulip and daffodil bulbs and iris rhizomes that would light up the little flower garden next spring. Trees must be protected from the frost. Tools needed mending. He also had to live up to the expectations of the King, who before going back to Paris had come to him and said, "I shall of course be counting on you, Monsieur de La Quintinie, to send me a selection of your best fruit and vegetables as often as possible." Three times a week hundreds of baskets, hampers and racks were dispatched to the Louvre palace, where the whole court had halted on its way to Saint-Germain-en-Laye.

→-◄-

Despite the distance and the preoccupations that kept him from the château at Versailles, the monarch still worried about how the seeds and young shoots were doing there. "How is your work going, Monsieur de La Quintinie?" he asked in a letter. "Do as I asked Monsieur Colbert to do – write to me at length, send me all the details about everything. I want you too to talk to me about my Versailles."

So in the evening the gardener wrote long screeds to the King. He described the slow metamorphoses taking place in both the château and the garden; the new species that foreign horticulturists had sent him recently and that he would soon be growing to please His Majesty. "The labourers are working now at the espalier gardens where the new peach trees are to be planted. In the west we are building new glasshouses for the fig trees. The work is making good progress and by next spring, with God's help, the garden will be capable of producing twice as much as before." He interspersed his enthusiasms as a gardener with his regrets as a courtier: he missed His Majesty, "who knew and loved so many things".

→>−<+

La Quintinie had kept the best of his staff – less than a dozen – with him. A few succinct instructions were all they needed to set to work digging in fresh manure, strengthening frames and greenhouses, preparing the soil and the seed-beds. With such helpers to rely on, he felt free, some afternoons, to take time off and go for long walks through the surrounding countryside.

Muffled up in a loose coat, his hands in his pockets, he would stroll along the Grand Canal, which was often shrouded in mist. On the right bank the three masts of the Great Galley rose up through the haze; further on lay the vague shapes of deserted rowing boats and gondolas. Sometimes La Quintinie would sit down on a cold stone bench. The winter-bound vessels seemed to be waiting for the sky to clear at last and the ice to loosen its grip on their hulls. He thought of his garden and his seeds and the sap in his trees: they too must be looking forward to their coming liberation. Then he would get up and turn to his left, making for the Menagerie and its attendant flocks of crows. Behind him the imposing mass of the château dissolved amid the over-arching branches.

→>-<-

The peasants were used to seeing him pass with his curious gait through their fields of wheat and rye. He examined the earth and the sky in the same way as they did. Some overcame their shyness and approached him, hat in hand. Gradually tongues were loosened, and country folk asked where the King was now and what he planned to do. They talked of the beauty of the château, of the spectacular entertainments held there, and of the lovely women they'd glimpsed the previous summer. Then their interest in the land reasserted itself, and the talk turned to crops and harvests. The peasants and La Quintinie exchanged seeds, some of which were heavy as lead; they debated the best way of planting turnips or cabbages.

La Quintinie liked being with these men. The doors of their cottages were open to him at any time of the day, and they would all chat and drink together amid the bleating of sheep and the clucking of poultry.

The peasants seldom complained of the poverty and uncertainty of their lives or of the onerous taxes they had to pay. They concentrated instead on how to increase their yields or ward off the vicissitudes of winter.

"My seedlings are eaten up with frost, and so are old Bernier's," one of them would say. "We haven't got enough manure – there's only one horse among three of us. He couldn't produce enough dung for us all even if we bored another hole in his backside!"

"How much would it cost to buy another horse?"

"A good one? Sixty livres at least – as much as three cows or twenty sheep. Only the ploughmen can afford to buy horses."

"Mix some chestnut or hornbeam leaves into your manure," La Quintinie advised them. "It will give out less heat, but the heat will last longer. And bank up the earth round your more delicate crops."

As the gardener spoke he filled the pages of his notebooks with sketches and diagrams.

"And what about weeds?"

"Spread old manure that's been used before over your fields. You can also use the residue that's left after apples or grapes have been pressed to make cider or wine."

"That's all very well, but you'd have to get up pretty early to find any!"

"I'll bring you some next time I come. And if you want to grow bigger marrows, mix some crushed broad beans in with your fertiliser."

They would go on talking like that for hours, sometimes until nightfall. Then the woman of the house would serve a thick soup which they'd eat out of bowls balanced on their knees or set on the corner of a table, sitting by a smoking fire with the children asleep nearby. The time passed peacefully. There was no more talking.

It was often late when La Quintinie left, smelling of grease

[14]

and soot. As he made his way home he gazed at the stars in their courses, forming patterns as swift and as frail as bean tendrils.

→>-<←

The news reaching Versailles from Paris was of more battles. Amid the snows of the Vosges, Turenne was leading twenty-five thousand men in yet another attempt to save Alsace by pushing back the army of the Great Elector of Brandenburg. Comments flew between the rows of marrows in the garden at Versailles.

"It'll never end!" said one of the workers.

"Nothing ever ends, Louis," answered another. "As you know full well, everything has to be done over and over again. What Turenne is trying to do there is exactly what you're trying to do here: one day you get the better of the weeds, and the next they're back and you have to fight them all over again."

"Yes, but what about all those casualties?"

"Everything has to be paid for, Louis. Isn't that right, Jean-Baptiste?"

The gardener didn't answer: he was thinking of a young man called Courtal who, armed with a flint-lock he didn't really know how to use, went off one July morning talking cheerfully of easy victories and a soldier's pay. His father had watched with pride as he marched away: his own son was going to help the great military strategists save the kingdom. But since then there had been no news of him. Everyone thought the boy must be dead. But this, instead of shattering the father, seemed to increase his stature. People came, sometimes from miles around, to admire him as he exulted, dry-eyed, at having "given his blood for France". La Quintinie wondered what would happen if one day the son suddenly reappeared.

III

"I shan't be away long," the gardener told his assistants. "A week at most."

Two days earlier he'd had a letter from the King. "There are people here," it said, "who miss you and insist on seeing you. And if you came you could get to know the city. Why not take advantage of the fact that there'd be room for you in Monsieur Dorbay's coach next week, when he comes to town to report to me on his work? And don't forget to bring me some of the new fruit you're so clever at inventing."

The prospect of Paris held little charm for La Quintinie. For one thing he didn't like leaving his garden. For another – and this was perhaps the main reason – he felt ill at ease in the city. He had seldom been to Paris. Most of what he knew of the capital he'd learned from reading Scarron and Boileau. They often referred to the narrowness of the streets there, and the dirt, and he thought of it as a vast ant-hill swarming with footpads and fops – though you couldn't always tell one from the other. Moreover it would be horribly trying to spend a whole morning travelling in Dorbay's company. He was the successor to La Quintinie's friend Le Vau, and the gardener often watched him showing off to his own little court, men and women, preening himself on plans and projects that weren't really his own. If he couldn't avoid Dorbay himself, though, perhaps he could avoid talking to him. But how? Should he affect to be asleep the whole way? Or pretend he'd suddenly lost his voice? On the morning they were due to set out he was still trying to think of something when Dorbay appeared, accompanied by two footmen laden with trunks and scrolls of parchment.

"Good day to you, Monsieur de La Quintinie," said he.

"Good day to you, Monsieur Dorbay," the gardener answered without thinking, only to realise he had ruined one of his chances. He racked his brains as they both got into the coach.

But by the time they'd gone a mile or so Dorbay, who said he was worn out by nights of work and pleasure, had fallen into a deep slumber.

To La Quintinie the journey across the plains under a frosty sky seemed endless. He was chilled to the marrow despite all the rugs he was wrapped in. His feet hurt horribly. If only he could talk it might take his mind off the cold . . . He was tempted a thousand times to shake his tedious travelling companion awake, but Monsieur Dorbay didn't come to until they had gone through the Porte d'Orléans.

➤➤◄◄

Peering as best he could through the chinks in the curtains of the coach, the gardener could only guess at rather than observe the scenes they were passing through. Judging by the noise the coach must be surrounded by a huge crowd: the shouting and bawling of carters, the cries of water-sellers and peddlers of almanacs, the squalling of infants, the screeches of women. The poets — Scarron and Boileau — had not been lying.

How long had they been crossing the city? On and on they still went. La Quintinie drew aside the curtain, and it seemed as if space had suddenly closed in around them. On either side of the street the coach was all but grazing walls of wood or stone. From doorways and windows issued hurrying forms and muffled voices. Watching the crowds floundering through the ill-lit muddy alleys, La Quintinie wondered, "What fate or magic spell keeps all these people cooped up here? Why do they stay in a place where there are no seasons or colours? Do they lead better lives than the peasants around Versailles? It's true it's very tough and primitive there, but it's free and untrammelled – it's on a human scale, the same scale as men's legs and arms, their vision and their souls."

A bend in a murky street gave La Quintinie a glimpse of a brighter scene, along the banks of the Seine. An icy wind had taken possession of that broad corridor, driving most citizens into the shelter of narrow lanes. There were carts and carriages everywhere, drawn by steaming horses. Their own coach turned in through a covered gateway and drew up at last in the courtyard of the Louvre. Dorbay smoothed out the creases in his breeches and straightened the hat he wore on top of his wig.

"Good day to you, then, Monsieur de La Quintinie," he said.

"And good day to you, monsieur," the gardener replied, turning on his heel and marching off into the palace without more ado. But his cold feet played him false, he tripped over a step, and only managed to save himself by clutching at the arm of a passing footman.

→>-<-

The corridors of the Louvre were almost indistinguishable from those of Versailles. They were just as crowded, full of the same confused shouting and laughter, the same hubbub of workmen, merchants and harassed lackeys, the same animal warmth. After the chill solitude of earth and sky, the gardener felt oppressed by it all. There was a terrible stench made up of urine, sweat and perfumes of various kinds. He could scarcely breathe.

"Hallo there, La Quintinie! So you're here at last!"

A big man, red-faced despite several layers of powder, emerged from a small group of people.

"Good day, Monsieur Dancourt."

The newcomer was probably one of the most eccentric characters at court. For several years his ungainly figure and tall wig had made him stand out amongst the rest. He could always be heard holding forth in the corridors and galleries during the day, and in the banqueting rooms at night. His passion for gambling was legendary. He was always the first to put his money down as soon as the tables were open, and his drinking was in direct proportion to his losses. "A hundred livres to the glass," he would jest. He usually went on playing until he was too drunk to count how many glasses he'd drunk. People soon came to the conclusion that he deliberately avoided winning. One evening when he'd lost more than seven thousand livres at a card game called *bassette*, the onlookers vied with one another to calculate, on the basis of Dancourt's own formula, the astronomical quantities of drink he must have put away in the process. Where did his money come from? How was it his excesses hadn't killed him yet? It was rumoured that because of some obscure family connection the King took care of his enormous debts and had him looked after by his own personal physician. The esteem shown for him by the King combined with his own joviality had won Dancourt some loyal friends – as well as some bitter enemies to whom he paid little attention.

"So, my old hermit, you've finally abandoned your own territory? Some of your friends had come to think your garden was more demanding than a mistress! But this morning I was told you were coming, and I've been lying in wait. You're just the person we need! Did you know the King was giving a fancy-dress ball this evening in the Salle des Caryatides?"

"No, I didn't know."

"Of course not, of course not … but I do hope you'll be there?"

"I really don't know. Apart from anything else, I'd have to find a costume."

"Come as you are!" Dancourt laughed. "With those rustic clothes and your hair like a haystack you're in fancy dress already."

La Quintinie blushed. He straightened his wig, smoothed the skirts of his coat and looked ruefully at the scratches on his hands and the earth lingering under his fingernails. Dancourt let out a guffaw.

"Come, come, man – I was joking! There's nothing wrong with you. But with your permission I'll find you something to wear tonight – something suitable for a man in your position. Do you know what rooms they've put you in? Not yet? Well then, meet me here in about an hour and I'll have everything you need."

✦✦✦

The apartments allotted to La Quintinie were on the top floor of the château and very cramped. A tiny window looked out on to the Cour Carrée. A small fire struggled to generate some warmth. The furniture consisted of a chest of drawers with a candlestick and a jug and basin on top; a little table with a stool; and a bed with hempen sheets and coarse woollen blankets. There were a couple of garish daubs on the wall depicting spring. But the gardener didn't mind. He scarcely noticed the lack of comfort. And hadn't he heard that others had been assigned even more meagre quarters, where it was impossible even to stand upright? He took off his hat and wig and put another log on the fire. The wood was damp and started to smoke.

A light knock on the door interrupted his solitude. Two footmen delivered his trunks. One of them handed him a note. The King couldn't leave his study now. "But I'll see you tomorrow towards the end of the morning. Meanwhile, amuse yourself looking over the palace. Go anywhere you like. I hope we shall have the pleasure of your company at the ball this evening. I understand Monsieur Dancourt is seeing to everything." News spread fast here.

La Quintinie dismissed the footmen, who turned up their noses at the tip he offered them. Was he supposed to hang about here in the cold? He put on his wig again and made for the galleries, from which a steady murmur of voices could be heard.

->-<-

He passed through a number of vast well-lit galleries, then through some narrower, darker corridors that suddenly opened into even vaster and brighter galleries than before, with even higher ceilings, though they were often crowded and stuffy.

"Look who's here!" someone suddenly cried. "Monsieur de La Quintinie! What a surprise! Come, my friends, let me introduce you to a man who gives delight to the King and to us all."

La Quintinie recognised the Comte de Namour, accompanied by two of his friends. Namour was undoubtedly one of the King's most inventive courtiers. One story about him in particular had done the rounds of all the royal residences. It told how a few years ago the count used to accompany the King every day on one of his favourite rides through the country around Versailles. Every time he did so the King would complain about the way a certain small wood spoiled the look of the park surrounding the château. Namour had a brilliant idea. One night he arranged for the offending trees to be sawn down by torch-light: every trunk was severed a quarter of the way up from its roots. Ropes were then tied to the branches and a servant put in charge of each rope. Next day as the King rode by the wood and was repeating his usual strictures, Namour rode up beside him and said:

"Sire, with your permission it would give me great pleasure to make the wood disappear."

"Proceed," said the King.

Namour snapped his fingers and the forest was promptly felled.

"Very amusing," commented the King, riding on.

→>-<←

"It really is a great pleasure to meet you here, Monsieur de La Quintinie," enthused Namour. "Allow me to present my old friends Monsieur le Comte d'Ardeville and Madame la Comtesse, who have just arrived here at the Louvre. They know you very well already — I've told them so much about you!"

"Monsieur de La Quintinie!" exclaimed d'Ardeville, proffering a limp hand. "I've been looking forward for a long time to meeting you and telling you how much I admire you. Monsieur de Namour has spoken to us so often about you and your work and what you are doing at Versailles. Extraordinary! Magnificent!"

"And your peas, my dear Monsieur, your peas!" cried his wife. "I'm told they're quite exquisite! I haven't yet had the pleasure of tasting them, but I hear such good things about them . . . But how do you manage to get the little things to grow in the middle of winter? You must have a secret. Do tell!"

"Well . . ."

"You haven't tasted his marrows yet, either!" put in Namour.

"I had an opportunity, not long ago, at the King's own table, to sample a marvellous soup . . ."

"Really?" said the gardener, faintly.

"When I think of the life you lead," said Madame d'Ardeville with a sigh, "out in all weathers in the sun and the mud and the cold! I really do admire you. But won't you tell me your secret? I have a small garden myself – a modest affair, but it gives me a lot of pleasure. Last year I managed to grow two pumpkins and some tomatoes. And now I'd love to succeed with some peas. I'd be so interested to learn your secret – I swear I wouldn't breathe a word of it to anyone else."

"Well . . ."

"Come, come, my dear, you can see you're embarrassing him. And of course he's not going to tell you anything." Namour came over to the gardener now and put a hand on his shoulder. "But Monsieur d'Ardeville is quite right. Nor can Madame be blamed for wanting to ferret out your mysteries. Only yesterday evening I was talking about you with Madame la Marquise de Réaumont. You are among the best practitioners of your art, if not the very best. Monsieur Morin can't hold a candle to you . . ."

"Morin? Who's he?"

"Louis Morin is a botanist like yourself. He's a member of the Academy of Sciences and from what I hear he's working at a new science that's supposed to be able to forecast the weather."

That was all Namour knew. So who, wondered the gardener, was this man whose work, if Namour's information was correct, might be very useful indeed?

"Might we come to see you one day at Versailles?" asked d'Ardeville. "My wife and I would be most interested to see you at work."

"Perhaps, while we're here, I might take the opportunity to

learn from you," the lady went on. "You will be my teacher, won't you?"

"Please be good enough to excuse me," La Quintinie suddenly blurted out. "I must go. Good day, madame. By your leave, gentlemen."

"No, no!" cried Madame d'Ardeville, grabbing him by the arm. "I won't let you go until you've told me your secret!"

"Now, now, my dear," he heard the husband say as he fled. "We'll go and see him soon at Versailles. He'll tell us how he does it in the end . . ."

→>—<←

In his haste to get away the gardener rushed through corridors and galleries without knowing where he was going. Finally he realised he was lost. He tried to retrace his steps, but the footmen and guards he asked for directions all told him something different. He didn't even consider consulting the courtiers: they seemed in such a hurry and so absorbed in their conversations. He caught another glimpse of Namour, and Madame d'Ardeville waved at him, but he strode on all the faster. Where on earth was he? He was reminded of the maze, ornamented with thirty-nine fountains, that Le Nôtre had recently designed.

"It's easy to get out of the maze there," he thought. "Le Nôtre claims it's impossible not to get lost, but all you need to do to find the way out is take a bearing on the sun and see which side of the hedge has been weathered by the wind and the rain."

But here there was no sun, wind or rain — only polished stone and marble floors. Everything was as smooth as a frozen river, and you couldn't tell which way it was flowing.

Then suddenly Dancourt, puffing and blowing like an ox that had just ploughed a heavy furrow, appeared round a bend in a corridor, and La Quintinie was saved.

"Found you at last!" cried the other. "I've been looking for you for over an hour. Where on earth have you been? Ah well, it doesn't matter now I've found you. Here are the things I promised you. I hope they fit."

And he handed over a parti-coloured suit, a wide belt, a hat, a pair of leather boots and a papier-mâché mask with a long sharp nose: a Harlequin costume. La Quintinie smiled. So this evening he was going to be cast as a comic character, a buffoon: that was natural enough. But why the mask? Harlequin didn't wear one in the theatre.

"But here it's the rule," Dancourt explained. "All the men are supposed to be anonymous until Canto –"

"Canto?"

"Charles Canto, the King's crier . . . Until the King gives a signal and Canto orders everyone to remove their masks. Just wait – you'll see how entertaining it can be. But now please excuse me – I must go and get ready."

The mask was amazing with its enormous nose, bright red mouth, prominent cheekbones and two hypnotic black holes for eyes.

"It'll be a clever man who recognises me this evening!" said the gardener, smiling. Then: "But tell me, Dancourt, which way should I go to . . . ?"

But Dancourt had mysteriously vanished.

*

With the aid of a young page La Quintinie finally found his way back to his rooms. The costume fitted him perfectly. What was it Sganarelle said? Oh yes!: "You don't understand Latin, monsieur?" "No." "*Cabricias, arci thuram, catalamus, singulariter, nominativo haec musa 'the Muse', bonus, bona, bonum, Deus sanctus, estne oratio latinas . . ."* He felt rather an impostor himself.

But by now he was prepared to be amused by his first few hours at the Louvre. Even Madame d'Ardeville's silliness made him smile. If he had to be in Paris he might as well make the most of it! The garden's in safe hands, he thought. And it's no bad thing to leave occasionally what you love best. Dancourt's right. I'm an old hermit.

When he heard the coaches of the first guests clattering into the courtyard, he put on his mask and hurried out of his apartments.

→>−<←

A buzz of voices surged up to meet him as he drew near the ballroom, and with it the heady perfumes of the ladies, the bitter smell of wax and the even stronger reek of torches dipped in tallow. La Quintinie went towards a pair of wide-open doors flanked by two Swiss guards. Then suddenly, in the glow of hundreds of candelabras redoubled by their reflections on walls of marble and gold, he saw hundreds of heads bedecked with feathers, wigs and hats of all shapes and sizes. For a moment he shrank back, afraid to join that outlandish throng, but a noisy group came up behind him and unceremoniously swept him along with them, and he was soon swallowed up in a maelstrom of heat, noise and light.

→>−<←

He felt more at ease once he was well into the room and surrounded by other people. His disguise made him completely unrecognisable and he was careful not to walk in his usual distinctive manner. As he moved anonymously among the groups of courtiers he caught sight of the King, accompanied by Monsieur and Madame – Louis' eldest brother, the Duc d'Orléans, and his wife the Duchesse. All three were wearing half-masks as, surrounded by an escort of pages and with the aid of lofty looks, impatient gestures and canes, they made their way through the crowd to places set apart for them. The gardener marvelled at the costumes and the imagination of the tailors and seamstresses who'd made them. He listened to a mustachioed Turk trying to convince a paint-bedaubed savage of the advantages of smoking tobacco and drinking coffee. He joined in the laughter of some pretty young ladies dressed as gardeners. More and more often he asked the footmen for goblets of strong wine, cursing the narrow mouth of his mask when it made him spill the precious drops down his collar instead of his throat.

"Good party, eh?"

"I dare say, monsieur, I dare say."

A doctor in a tall wig and carrying a huge syringe was talking to a horned devil.

"A very intimidating costume . . ."

"It cost me a small fortune. I'm quite pleased with the effect."

"I should think so!"

"But some of the others are very good too. Look at that Armenian with the huge moustache. You'd think he'd come straight from Erevan."

"Yes indeed."

"Isn't he the Marquis de Tabard?"

"What wonderful intuition!"

"It's not intuition, doctor – it's physiology! I'd recognise the Marquis anywhere. That awkward walk, those fluttery gestures, and the stoop! Yes, it must be him – it's impossible to conceal such lumpishness."

"He may be cleverer than we think."

The Devil burst out laughing.

[27]

"It's easy to see you don't know the Marquis! Believe me, he doesn't know the meaning of grace or subtlety."

"Are you sure?"

"Certain. Everyone at court says the same."

"Everyone?"

"Absolutely everyone. Haven't you heard about his latest scrape? One evening about a week ago he insisted on seeing the King to the royal apartments. He grabbed a torch from one of the pages to clear a way through the crowd and laid about him with such enthusiasm he set the King's wig on fire!"

"And what's the King's opinion of him, then?"

"I'm told he steers clear of the arsonist if he can, and so does everyone else, naturally. The Marquis's career is over. This is probably about the last time we shall see him at court, if not his very last appearance."

And then, as if by tacit accord, the crowd fell silent. La Quintinie turned instinctively towards the end of the room where an orchestra was taking its place on a platform. There was some applause, then after the musicians had settled down they were joined by a man carrying a long staff.

"That's Lully!" someone whispered.

"Are you sure?" said another. "I can't see a thing through this wretched mask."

"Yes, it's him. It's Lully."

"Do you know what Monsieur de La Fontaine says about him?" asked a woman. "He says he's very lewd and is always making bawdy remarks."

"They say he was once baker's boy to the Grande Duchesse! But you must admit his music is divine!"

Lully bowed to the King and raised his baton, and the first notes of *Alceste* wafted through the audience, making their way between Turks and savages, above the tall hats of physicians and among the little huddles of pretty "gardeners". The music left La Quintinie in transports of delight. His eyes flew up to the frescoed ceiling, sped down the Doric columns, whirled round with the dancers, rose up again to the friezes. Then he was suddenly struck by a detail – a small medallion on the wall, surrounded by paintings of warlike scenes. Within the little medallion La Quintinie caught sight of woods, a river, steep valleys, clouds. And behind these he seemed to see images of the château at Versailles and the outlines of tall trees. The voices of peasants seemed to reach him, the smell of the earth and of his garden – his own garden, so small and far away, which for a little while had been obliterated by a few showy garments and bits of coloured paper. Then the heat in the room became unbearable, the sound turned into meaningless din, the lights grew pale, Lully and his staff disappeared. La Quintinie made for the door, tearing off his mask.

As he went along the dark corridor leading to his room he all at once became aware of a vague shape close beside him. Before it could vanish through a doorway, the gardener thought he recognised the doctor who earlier in the evening had been talking with the Devil. Voices followed the physician's retreating form.

"Monsieur le Marquis de Tabard, where are you off to? Come back!"

IV

The gardener awoke with a bitter taste in his mouth. He knew it wasn't only because of the quantities of wine he'd drunk the night before. He had a feeling that somehow during the evening he'd done something wrong or failed in some duty, and that Providence would make him pay dearly for it.

As he dressed he thought back with surprise on how quickly he'd let himself be caught up in the frivolities of a world to which he knew he didn't belong. He'd imagined he was free, protected by his love of nature, but hadn't he left his work and come running at a mere sign from the King, just like all the other courtiers? Hadn't he allowed himself to be drawn against his will into this great labyrinth of gildings and paintings and marble statues, this world of artifice where everyone was doomed to get lost? What yesterday had seemed just a misadventure was swiftly turning into a nightmare. He both marvelled and quailed at the thought that one man could have gathered around him, and could have enslaved and muzzled, so many men and women. He recalled glances and looks he had merely glimpsed the previous evening – eyes imploring a glance in return or a gesture from the King, a sign which if he deigned to vouchsafe it would justify someone's whole existence.

He tried to reassure himself.

"But *I* could have declined the King's invitation if I'd wanted to. And he needs me just as much as I need him."

He wanted desperately to believe in such mutual dependency as proof that he really was free.

He was shivering as he went over to the window: there'd been a heavy fall of snow during the night. The big ornamental pond was frozen over and servants crossing the icy courtyard found it hard to stay upright, no doubt to the amusement of the few courtiers already about at this hour. La Quintinie thought of his garden far away, and his naked plants suffering as he did from the cold. Had his men taken all the proper precautions? Had they got out the thick hempen covers he kept for use in such weather? They'd probably forgotten to mend the five broken windows in the main glasshouse. Had his farmers solved their manure problem? What was he himself doing here when everything cried out for him there?

There was a knock at the door. Before he could answer, the massive figure of Dancourt loomed on the threshold. It was obvious he'd been up all night: his carnival wig drooped pitifully over his right eye; his habitual heavy make-up had melted under the mask and ran down his face in streaks; an expanse of wine-stained white linen shirt hung out of one side of his suit where it had come unhooked. Behind him stood a tall stranger.

"La Quintinie!" cried Dancourt, as lively as ever despite his sleepness night. "We've been looking for you for hours! Finally a footman told us where your rooms were. But where on earth did you vanish to yesterday evening? You must be a magician to be able to disappear into thin air like that. Anyhow, you really missed something. You should have seen the Marquise de Brinvilliers . . ."

"I'm sure you found plenty to amuse you," La Quintinie replied tersely.

Dancourt slumped down onto the bed. The stranger was still standing by the door. Dancourt seemed suddenly to remember his presence.

"You don't seem to recognise our friend, La Quintinie."

"I must admit . . ."

"But he knows you very well. At least so he told me yesterday evening, and when I told him this morning that I was going to look for you he insisted on coming with me."

"Forgive me, monsieur," said La Quintinie, turning towards the person in question, "but I'm afraid I really can't place you."

"Well, it's a very long time since we met. I'm Philippe – Philippe de Neuville."

"Good heavens! Philippe! What miracle brings you here?"

Neuville had changed a great deal since he had finished his legal studies at the university. His features were harder; his face, framed by a mop of hair, had grown very thin. He'd spent several years as a lawyer, then turned his attention to astrology, astronomy and science. He was particularly interested in alchemy, and in one of its most important applications, the making of bread. He had written a number of books that had created a stir in advanced circles, and was about to publish an article in a Dutch newspaper on Olaüs Römer, a Danish astronomer working on some abstruse problems concerning the speed of light. But what took up all his time at the moment was a pamphlet he was writing against a scheme for setting up a Conversion Fund to pay Protestants for abjuring their faith.

"I'm not a Protestant myself," he said, "but such spiritual tyranny is inadmissible! How far will intolerance go? We must be ceaselessly on our guard, messieurs. I don't care if La Reynie and his secret police do come after me! I shall put my name on the pamphlet. I'm not afraid of them! I'm not afraid of anyone!"

He'd arrived in Paris three days before to sort out a complicated case concerning a legacy. The affair had been settled and he was due to leave this evening for Orléans to visit a countess in delicate health who had nevertheless become quite a serious student of alchemy.

"That leaves us a few hours to see the sights of Paris together," said Dancourt.

"I have to see the King this morning," said La Quintinie, "and I don't know how long the interview will last."

"We could wait for you," said Dancourt. "The King is completely preoccupied by the situation in Alsace. They say Turenne is held up by the snow. Condé is supposed to be going to help him. I'm prepared to wager your audience won't last long."

→>-<←

On that cold January morning the gardener paced up and down outside the King's study. At last a door opened and an usher came over to him and said:

"His Majesty cannot receive you for the moment. But he hopes to see you at supper. Be here again this evening at ten."

V

The sharp cold air made lungs burn and hands tingle. Clouds flew towards the plain over the snow-covered roofs. In what direction was Versailles? Did his garden lie in the distance beyond this building, or in a line parallel with that? Neither Neuville nor Dancourt could tell him.

The cobblestones were slippery and the three men had to hold on to one another at every step for safety. After what seemed to the gardener like hours, they halted.

"Here we are," Neuville told the others. "This, my dear friends, is probably the greatest work that man, inspired by God, has ever created."

The forced march was over, and La Quintinie could raise his head at last. What he saw took his breath away. Before him a vast edifice rose out of the depths of the earth and stretched up to the sky in two tall towers. His head thrown back to take in the extraordinary prospect, La Quintinie felt quite dizzy. Slowly he lowered his eyes past the rose window, the tympanum showing Christ in glory, then the rows of sculptures separated by columns, until at last he was on solid earth again, looking at the crowd of pilgrims. The voice of Neuville brought him back to reality.

"Look at that fascinating world of symbols! A Bible in stone!" The pamphleteer sounded as though he'd helped to build the place himself. "Do you see that woman on the right there, sitting holding a sceptre and two books, and that ladder with nine rungs, the nine stages in the process of alchemy? Have you ever seen anything like it?"

La Quintinie tried to take in what his enthusiastic guide was saying, but suddenly he heard no more. His imagination had escaped over the roofs and was fleeing across the country to the trees at Versailles, his trees, living structures of sap and leaves and fruit and birds of every hue, his trees that were nature's masterpieces, never to be equalled by any architect.

That evening La Quintinie availed himself of Neuville's coach to return to Versailles. He had sent a letter to the King explaining that urgent matters called him back to the garden, humbly craving His Majesty's forgiveness, and assuring him of his deep devotion.

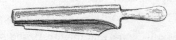

VI

The King had forgiven him. He probably had better things to do anyway than to scold a gardener whose work gave him complete satisfaction. It was January 1675 and Turenne had just defeated the army of the Elector of Brandenburg at Turckheim. Defeated was not exactly the word: one morning as the French troops were preparing to charge, a scout came in and announced that the Germans had vanished into thin air during the night. They looked everywhere but all they found were traces of the enemy camp with smoking embers and corpses abandoned under an empty sky. But no enemy soldiers. Turenne had gone back to Saint-Germain-en-Laye, where he had to be given a hero's welcome. Father Mascaron officiated at what would have been a splendid mass if his sermon hadn't declared that heroes were thieves who accomplished at the head of an army what ordinary robbers carried out unaided. The King sent for him after the service and told him: "I am responsible not to men but to God. And you, Monsieur Mascaron, despite your title, are only a man."

Since then Louis the Great had gone to the wars once more at the head of the Church as well as of an army of thousands. On the now weakened German frontier he set an example to all. In breastplate and helmet and mounted on a big bay horse he captured fort after fort amid a turmoil of shouting and ruins. And the ladies invited to view the show applauded from their dais the gallantry of a warrior king who still found time in the evening to organise the camp and the sentries and to eat and drink heartily.

→>-<←

The gardener had quietly resumed his place in his garden. But he still had a vague memory of the lights of the Louvre and of the courtiers in masks of powder or papier-mâché – all those people imprisoned behind walls of gold or marble or plaster, shut up in a noisy world without aim or object, crowding together, exchanging words and looks and gestures yet destined never to meet.

He himself was never alone: his garden was forever summoning him, soliciting his every look and action and thought. The smallest thing could lead to either triumph or disaster. He had to be there all the time, obeying the whims of a demanding Nature, accepting victory and defeat with equanimity. Slowly the garden was changing, and so was the man.

→>-<←

To the west new plots were patiently cleared and got ready for use. Onions and carrots were sown and grown in hotbeds; more rows of apple, peach and pear trees were planted side by side to encourage one another to be fruitful.

Now the garden was bursting with colour and energy, its surface decked with leaves round or serrated, with petals, tendrils and blossoms, while in the dark depths of the earth or amid the branches each fruit and vegetable grew into its final shape before emerging into the sight of men.

→>-<←

The news spread like wildfire: Turenne had met his death on 27th July 1675 on the right bank of the Rhine. The circumstances of the event remained obscure, but the population at large were convinced the great man had died after an epic and bloody struggle against the enemy. The leaderless French army had retreated for a while before the imperial troops, and the whole court was gripped once more by the fears of last summer. Would the Grand Condé, who'd been sent to the front, be able to reverse the situation?

Another subject of debate was the Marshal's funeral. People said the ceremonies would match the man himself and his valour. The King even contemplated burying him beside Du Guesclin among the royal tombs at Saint-Denis. The monument was to be a splendid affair made of the finest stone and marble, with a granite coffin placed inside a tower decorated with coats of arms and surrounded by statues and enormous trees. Everyone marvelled at this grandiose project. So complex was its symbolism that Ménestrier, who was responsible for building it, had a little book of explanations printed.

Like everyone else La Quintinie heard of this *castrum dolorosis*, this granite edifice put up to celebrate a man's glory and a King's power. He too had read the famous letter in which Madame de Sévigné rhapsodised over Turenne's sudden and providential death. "What more could he have wished for?" she asked. "He died in the midst of his glory. His reputation could not have grown any greater. Sometimes, when a man lives on, his star fades." But whenever anyone in his garden ventured to comment on the matter, La Quintinie said nothing. He thought it absurd to pile up all that stone just to hold a decaying corpse. "Turenne," he often mused, "didn't make the world. All he did was extend or defend frontiers invented by men. All he planted in the earth were cannon balls, thousands of cannon balls which devastated the land, smashed trees, rent clouds and crushed men and insects alike. His elaborate tomb is like his life: pointless. It's the lowly folk he left to rot on the battlefields, men whose names are forgotten, who made the world and go on doing so. As their bodies decay they break up and filter down to the farthest recesses of the earth, feeding roots and insects deep in the dark, which one day will bring us news of the world below."

And then he would think of young Courtal, whose life was now fed by sap and humus and rose towards the sky in the form of a stem or stalk, its petals opening to the gentle warmth of a new day.

VII

The Grand Condé was victorious and the court had resumed its trials and tribulations. The King was on the road again between Chantilly, Saint-Germain, the Louvre and — more and more often — Versailles. Every time there was the same harnessing of horses, the same frenzied arrivals and departures, the same long procession of coaches and wagons. In the midst of all the to-ing and fro-ing the King seemed indefatigable. The memorialists were always singing the praises of his remarkable constitution. Hardly had he arrived at Versailles than he would shut himself up in his study, send for his advisers and architects, now checking the measurements of a window, then strolling round and delighting in his garden, accompanied by Le Nôtre and a court trying to conceal its exhaustion.

Of course he never failed to visit La Quintinie and ask how the work was going. The gardener gladly did the honours, pointing out here a new plant with which he was particularly pleased and there another that was a disappointment. The King was extremely interested in all the gardener had to say. Several times he was even seen wielding a rake for an hour or two with a straw hat on his head and an apron round his waist, puffing and blowing just like an ordinary labourer. Then the gardener would marvel that a man who could subdue whole cities and had the power to decide the fate of thousands at a glance should be so careful and patient with plants and herbs in a little garden.

→►◄←

One August morning the King sent for him.

"You know, of course, my dear La Quintinie," he said, "that Condé has recently won a famous victory. Such a brilliant demonstration of the art of war should not and must not go unremarked. I should like, in honour of our hero and for the edification of the court, to organise a celebration really worthy of the name. Will you kindly select enough of your best fruit and vegetables to provide for, say, a thousand people? Everything must be ready in about four weeks."

"A thousand people, Sire? I'm afraid my garden isn't big enough to feed so many."

"I've been told you are a magician, Monsieur de La Quintinie," answered the King. "Don't disappoint me."

La Quintinie hastily called his staff together and divided up the work, at the same time handing out straw hats, flasks and tools. The gardeners, armed with billhooks, watering cans, rakes, hoes and forks, hurried from one plot to another, some looking after the cabbages, others tending the beans, salads and different kinds of fruit.

But it soon had to be admitted that the task was too great, and one morning La Quintinie went to see the King. Outside the royal bedchamber a crowd of gentlemen were already waiting to be received. Their conversation was so animated the ushers were often obliged to call for silence. Ignoring the disapproving looks and murmurs of other suitors, some of whom had been there several hours, La Quintinie went over to the head footman and demanded an audience. The footman whispered something to the chief gentleman of the bedchamber, who vanished through an inner door. He emerged again almost at once and signed to the gardener to follow him.

La Quintinie found the King being shaved in the presence of a small group of courtiers. As he bowed, the King, without turning his head, spoke to him.

"Well, my dear fellow, is the work making good progress?"

"Sire, that's just what I came to see you about. My magic will never be powerful enough to deliver all you ask on time. To do that I'd need fifty more men."

The King smiled.

"You shall have them, Monsieur de La Quintinie."

That afternoon the gardeners saw an army of liveried footmen arriving. The workmen laughed at the newcomers' uniforms and gave them all the most disagreeable tasks to do. The novices were slow and often incompetent, and curses rained on them from their reluctant colleagues.

→>—<←

For many long weeks the sky had been cloudless, and there wasn't enough water in the irrigation channels to keep the plants from wilting. The day labourers spent most of their time going back and forth between the garden and the reservoirs supplied from the pond at Clagny and the Montboron hills. La Quintinie himself joined in, observing that every time he dipped his jar in the tank the water level was lower. Dripping with sweat as he toiled back to the garden, he bemoaned not the size and demands of the world but his own human littleness and lack of power. The water he needed was the water the King had decided to use for ornamental ponds and fountains to amuse the court.

La Quintinie had raised the crucial question of irrigation with the King some years earlier, but the answer he received was full of pride and complacency.

"No need to worry, La Quintinie. At this very moment people are experimenting with various kinds of pump to draw water from the Seine, and with God's help their work will produce a regular supply not only for the inhabitants of the château itself but also for Monsieur Le Nôtre's gardens and fountains and of course for your own domain."

"Might I ask, Sire, when that project will be decided upon and begun?"

"Soon, my dear fellow, very soon."

Months, years had gone by, and the experiments had turned out to be too complicated and expensive to be put into practice. La Quintinie had had to learn to be satisfied with what he could get.

As he leaned over the dark surface of the tanks he often found himself thinking of the water's long journey. After falling from the sky and slowly making its way down to subterranean caves, it had remained underground for a long while, then worked its way upward through barriers of roots and stones. Now with a rustle as of leaves it came to the surface at last, looking up to a desperately rainless sky.

"The things that are most important are given to us for nothing," he reflected. "The rest — the things that money can buy — are worthless."

At last everything was ready. The south wing of the château was littered with crates and hampers. The paths that crisscrossed the garden had emptied as if by magic, and once more you could see into the distance, past the box hedges to the roots of heaven.

On the evening of the celebrations the gardener was nowhere to be found, though dozens of pages were sent to look for him.

VIII

Neuville had written, delighted at the way sheer chance had helped renew their friendship a few months earlier.

"I'm so happy to have found you again after all these years. I deplore the distance that keeps us apart, but treasure the memory of our meeting. May Heaven permit us to see one another again soon."

The articles that took up all his time and energy, he said, met with general indifference. But far from discouraging him, the silence that greeted each of his publications only encouraged him to persevere in the slow dissemination of knowledge. His pamphlet was exploring unexpected depths. But as he expected, it had come to the attention of Nicolas de La Reynie, chief of the Paris police, and Neuville had had to move house several times. On each occasion he'd been tracked down.

"But it's probably a good sign that I'm regarded as a nuisance. I must be on the right path: people don't scratch unless they itch."

Neuville also took a close interest in the revolt that had been threatening Brittany since the previous spring, taking the side of the poor people oppressed with new taxes imposed to finance the war effort and pay for the extravagances of supercilious nobles.

"No one really knows anything about the outrages that have been inflicted on the peasants in Brittany. They are hanged and tortured and raped one after the other. The soldiers enter the towns with their guns at the ready and their swords drawn, as if they were entering enemy territory. The people are being massacred, and everyone seems to think that's perfectly normal."

La Quintinie admired Neuville and the enthusiasm with which he espoused such causes, but he was anxious about his friend's future.

"Don't worry about me," Neuville told him. "Writing these articles gives my life a meaning at last. How many people can say as much nowadays?"

→>-<←

Dancourt had written too. He explained briefly that so far important business had prevented him from coming to Versailles. But chiefly he gave a curious description of court life in Paris, with its harassments and its gambling.

"Ever since the King acquired a passion for billiards everyone else here has followed suit. Without exception they've all been seen crouching over a table trying to make ivory balls collide with one another. Naturally, when the King himself plays everyone else does his best to cheat – not to win but to lose. And do you know – in Paris people are quarrelling over whether the inscription on the triumphal arch that's to be built in the Place du Trône should be in French or Latin! On one side are the Ancients and on the other the Moderns, and endless books are written on the subject, and meetings held in drawing rooms and cafés, and of course round billiard tables. People eat and drink and argue, imagining they're changing the world by hitting balls about and setting ancient Rome against modern France. But one of these days that whole world is going to have to be turned upside down."

What had become of Dancourt's impudent humour, his nonchalance, his love of gambling, his eagerness to embrace every new craze at court?

"One changes," he explained laconically when the gardener expressed surprise. "It's about time anyhow. Soon I'll be fifty years old."

But when La Quintinie asked what he meant by turning the world upside down, Dancourt gave no reply.

IX

Versailles always echoed with rumours, but one soon drove out all the others. The Marquise de Brinvilliers had been arrested three weeks ago in Liège.

"Who?"

"The Marquise de Brinvilliers."

"I don't believe it!"

"It's true, I tell you! Do you remember my cousin, André Chevallier?"

"Of course."

"Well, he works at the Châtelet with Monsieur Nicolas de La Reynie. He told me about it. He was even there when La Brinvilliers was questioned."

"But why was she arrested?"

"She's supposed to have used 'inheritance powder' to do away with her relations so as to get hold of their property herself."

"Incredible!"

"But that's not all. When she was put to the question she confessed she was taught how to make the powder by someone called Sainte-Croix, who killed himself by accident while concocting poison and who once tried to be taken on as butler to the King."

"You mean he wanted to murder him?"

"That's what the police think. But imagine if he'd managed to get the job ... ! We wouldn't be here talking about it now. And that's not the worst. My cousin says that extraordinary things happened when the Marquise was on the rack – flames shot out of her eyes and she spoke in a terrifying voice, a voice that wasn't her own, in a language no one could understand . . . Promise you won't tell anyone else about all this."

→>–<←

The arrest of La Brinvilliers and the fact that someone had plotted to harm the King's person – and by the same token also threatened the lives of some of his most illustrious courtiers – sent a wave of terror sweeping through Versailles, which La Reynie's heavy-handed methods only served to strengthen. No one talked of anything else but poisons, witchcraft and murders, and soon people were afraid to eat or drink or go out at night. They huddled at home as soon as it got dark, refused all invitations, and were suspicious of neighbours, servants, friends and relatives alike. They complained bitterly because the King was far away on the Flemish frontier and couldn't be on the spot to restore order and calm in his own kingdom.

→>–<←

For months the branches had almost imperceptibly been filling with sap. Then all of a sudden the trees were green. The big ships came into service again until the autumn, until the time drew near when storms would be too strong for them. All around La Quintinie the earth was cracking open, the first visible sign of the growth that was going on below. The gardener paid little attention to the worldly or military preoccupations of the court. He cared only for the seeds crying out for water, listened only to the plaint of the trees as their branches yearned upward.

→>–<←

Finally the King and Monsieur returned, wreathed in new glory. Everyone was relieved to learn that regardless of distance and despite the rigours of battle the King had kept himself informed daily of the Affair of the Poisons.

On 17th July 1676, La Brinvilliers' right hand was cut off in the porch of Notre-Dame. She was then beheaded and burned in the Place de Grève, in front of a crowd of courtiers making such a clamour that the *Salve Regina* sung at executions was inaudible.

But the general apprehensions, far from abating, only redoubled. It soon transpired that under interrogation the Marquise had given away many names. Hundreds of people, some of them courtiers, were involved in the Affair. It was the talk of the town and cast doubt on the omnipotence both of the King and of his police.

⤛⤜

The gardener was worried as well as interested by the news Neuville now sent him more and more regularly. His pamphlet had been seized and he and his Lyons publisher had both been threatened with imprisonment. The authorities had closed down their printing press, and a Conversion Fund had been introduced. "Six livres per recantation – that's what Monsieur Pellison proposes! The whole affair is disgusting. One thing is certain, though: there won't be many conversions at that price. But I shall go on fighting to the bitter end, no matter what the opposition."

He went on: "The year 1676 is a turning point. Römer has succeeded in calculating the speed of light by observing the satellites of Jupiter! Think of it: nearly seventy-seven thousand leagues a second! The world is full of surprises. Every year opens up new gulfs of perplexity and puts us in our proper place – as equals, all of us equal to one another in the face of what is beyond our understanding. Only if we go on believing we have some understanding of our own life and of the life that surrounds us shall we fail to be united. We must admit that some things are unknowable, accept that we are ignorant and helpless on this tiny ball of earth spinning around in the immensity of the sky. And this realisation should make us afraid. Every new discovery is salutary if it makes men despair of themselves.

"And you, my dear fellow, how are you? Knowing you are there is a great comfort to me in these hard times. Write to me. Don't forget your friend."

"I sympathise with all you say," replied the gardener. "Every day, looking at a plant, or at an insect creeping along the stem of a flower, I have thoughts very similar to yours. What can I, what can *we* understand of all this mechanism operating in apparent disorder yet in accordance with a logic of its own? I am equally terrified by the speed of your light and the slowness of my snails."

X

 It seemed as if winter would never end. Snow and frost gnawed away at the earth for month after month. Despite all the cloches, the daily applications of manure, the spreading of heavy canvas covers and the willing work of the labourers, it was impossible to maintain enough warmth to keep the seeds and the early spring shoots alive. Whole beds had to be uprooted and dispersed: the only thing to do was save what still had a chance of survival. The great greenhouses were crammed with trees in pots, fruit trees and such flowers and vegetables as had been able to resist the harsh weather.

La Quintinie was chiefly worried not for himself and his garden but for the peasants: every day their reserves shrank and their fears increased. Famine had filled the roads with poverty-stricken hordes who ransacked the labourers' meagre vegetable patches, killing the stock and sometimes even murdering their owners.

The kitchen garden itself was not unscathed. One night a gang of men scaled the walls, smashed the glass in the green-houses and stole the fruit, vegetables and tools inside. In the process they also trampled and wrenched out many other plants which they just left lying. Bontemps and his men were ordered to keep watch over the garden day and night. But the thieves did not return. La Quintinie could understand how hunger could lead men to do such things, but he deplored the pointless destruction that ruined his work. "If only they'd just come to see me ..."

Such dramatic events made people resent the recent departure of the King and Monsieur. A few weeks ago, on the night of Shrove Tuesday, the two of them had suddenly vanished only to reappear in the report of the next day's military activities, at the head of their troops, leading a new campaign in Flanders. Murmurs began to be heard to the effect that the Monarch would be better employed protecting his subjects instead of rushing to the ends of the earth to promote the greatness of France. And Versailles, scared, bereft of its King, huddled away deeper every day in the damp cold labyrinth of its vast marble corridors.

The hearts of the courtiers might be lightened and their courage revived for a day by the punishments frequently carried out on the parade ground. People might try to forget the horror of the situation by skating on the Grand Canal, hunting pheasants and deer (under suitable escort), applauding Lully's *Isis*, or arguing whether it was Racine or Pradon who was the first to slay Phèdre. But at dusk they went back to their apartments accompanied by armed pages, and before retiring for the night they looked under their beds to make sure no rough peasants, with their gaunt greedy hands, were lurking there.

→>◄←

In May 1676 the bands of marauders evaporated as swiftly as they had arrived. No one knew why. Some people believed the mysterious disappearance of the rebels coincided with the triumphal return of the King. Others put it down to months of energetic efforts on the part of Bontemps and his men. For others again the explanation lay simply in a decided improvement in the weather. But if the retreat of the bogeymen was a subject of debate, it was doubtless not so much because the courtiers wanted to find out the truth as because the question provided a useful topic of conversation.

The whole kingdom felt quiet and safe again. It was said the King would soon conclude a very favourable peace treaty with his enemies. With all his victories behind him he was in a position to impose his slightest whim on the rest of Europe. And the people of France marvelled at their good fortune in being ruled by a king whom the whole world admired and feared.

"How, after all they have suffered and will suffer still, can the people go on revering a man whose only object is excess? I confess I don't understand," wrote Neuville. "If you brand men with red-hot irons they will protest for a moment, but as time goes by very few of them seem to remember their wounds. Is everyone afflicted with amnesia? What *is* the explanation? What do all these people expect? Will their lives be changed for the better because their country inspires more fear than almost any other in Europe? It's as if we remember nothing of all we have learned. And that's what fills me with horror and consternation now."

Would the world never change, then? La Quintinie refused to accept that.

"Do you think the peasants who live around here don't dream of a better life?" he wrote. "They don't share your pessimism. What has become of my friend who used to say he'd go on fighting no matter what the opposition? I agree that at our level there isn't all that much we can do. But a few of us can at least try. And I'm sure your knowledge and my position should help us to get somewhere. Write again soon."

XI

 The rainstorms were less violent; the clouds streamed by more slowly. It was spring at last, and as the warm sap circulated, every living thing in the garden looked forward to the ordeal of its birth and the subsequent inevitability of its death.

→>—<—

The King, Madame and a few of the courtiers had once more gone off to the war. From Dunkirk to Brisach, Louis the Great at the head of a hundred thousand men set the Belgian countryside aflame and confirmed once and for all, for any who still had doubts, the might of his army. The siege of Ghent was the main subject of conversation in corridors and salons. The King's renown increased every day in the minds of sensation-seekers fed with carefully selected and edited reports. But above all, more and more often and more and more openly, people talked of Madame de Maintenon, whom certain ironic and far-seeing wits had nicknamed Madame de Maintenant.[*]

→>—<—

"Did you know, my dear Philippe, that before he went away the King made it known that he's decided to make Versailles his

[*] A pun suggesting that Madame de Maintenon's period in favour might be short-lived, *"maintenant"* meaning "now".

[55]

principal residence? It's no surprise to anyone here. But what nobody knows yet is exactly when it's going to happen. At the moment the château is quite uninhabitable. So a great series of operations is planned, directed by Monsieur Jules Hardouin-Mansart. A little while ago I myself had to leave my former garden and hand over the responsibility for it to Monsieur Vautier. In its place I've been given an area that in due course will be large enough to satisfy the Royal Appetite. It's the extensive earth-moving works recently undertaken in connection with this that have prevented me from writing to you sooner. Please don't be vexed. I can't pretend I'm not overjoyed to have a decent amount of new land at my disposal at last, where I'll be free to make all kinds of horticultural experiments."

The land now entrusted to La Quintinie was a rectangle covering some ten hectares at the bottom of Satory Hill. What the gardener didn't tell his friend was that the site had been chosen for aesthetic reasons rather than because of the qualities of the soil.

"I discussed the matter at length with Monsieur Hardouin-Mansart," the King had told him. "The main thing about this arrangement is that it will improve the view from what will eventually be the Southern Terrace."

The site had till then been no more than an insect-ridden swamp. On the other hand, its exposure to the sun was ideal, with enough local variation to grow many different kinds of crops. So La Quintinie said nothing. He would bring in new soil which he would then improve and enrich; he would dig channels, line them with stones and connect them to tanks. Mansart was going to help by building a surrounding wall. The King, quoting Quintilian, had assisted in the planning of the garden: "Is there anything more pleasing, my dear La Quintinie, than a space divided up in such a way that from whatever point of view you look at it you see only straight lines?"

"I dare say not, Sire."

The gardener followed the King's plans to the letter. The garden was to consist of a sunken central space divided into sixteen rectangles, with a circular pond in the middle. Around the sixteen inner plots were thirty or so outer rectangles of different sizes, separated by high dividing walls.

"In this space, which is perfectly designed and sheltered from the wind," La Quintinie wrote to Neuville, "I shall be able to grow whatever I like. I shall prune and shape my trees. I'm sure the fruit trees, exposed to the sun regularly and from all directions, will give of their best. It is a wonderful thing for me to be able to help build and improve all this."

But torrential rain often made the site revert almost to its former wild state

"Last week," the gardener lamented one day to Neuville, "there were so many downpours the whole place looked like a lake again, an impenetrable marsh fatal both to the recently planted trees and to the vegetables, which are submerged under inches of water."

It was often necessary to clean up the soil or bring in new loads of earth altogether. The drainage canals would have to be cleared, new ones added, crops replanted, mosquitoes warded off. The labourers railed against the awful working conditions and the backbreaking toil. "Nature has rights. We have only duties," La Quintinie would say, joining in as his men wheeled barrow after barrow of water-logged earth to and fro. "We'll build things up again every time it's necessary – that's what is asked of us. But everything we do should be performed as an act of humility."

→→←←

"Why," asked Neuville, "have you surrounded your garden with ramparts and separated all the plots with high walls? When I look at the plans you sent me I see nothing but partitions, compartments and perfectly straight paths. Forgive my frankness, my friend, but I can't understand all these barriers closing things in instead of letting them expand freely. Why do you cut yourself off from the universe just when it is beckoning to us, just when the world is growing larger before our very eyes and we are almost able to reach the stars?"

"I appreciate your frankness," the gardener replied. "The walls that you deplore I designed as supports for my fruit trees. I'll tell you soon about my methods here. But first and foremost the enclosed spaces were intended as shelters. You can't imagine how I enjoy being inside one of these little refuges, far away from everything, at any hour of the day or night. Inside each hidden kingdom everything *can* move freely: the grass as it pushes aside the flower that gets in its way, the slug as it crawls up a lettuce leaf, the grasshopper leaping from plant to plant, the ant hauling a seed along that's bigger than itself. And as I pore over these tiny universes, each greater far to me than all your galaxies, I myself cease to exist. When are you going to come here? Everything is waiting for you, and so am I."

→>-<+

Beyond the surrounding wall of the garden, more and more scaffolding was going up and crowds of workers were arriving from all over the country.

Mansart was working day and night. Colbert was shut up in his study raising new taxes.

"I hear the château is to be extended southward. The drawing rooms are to be altered. The long terrace between the King's and the Queen's apartments, which has always been damp, is to be covered in. Dorbay has just finished the great Ambassadors' Staircase."

For his part Le Nôtre had been encouraged to use as much as he wanted of the vast marshland opening on to the Galie valley.

"My confidence in you is boundless and the funds at your disposal are unlimited," the King had told him before going to Belgium. "Work! Work!"

So he worked, and read Bacon, Claude Mollet and Olivier de Serres. He drew up plans and ordered his men to dig and sow and prune endlessly. He surrounded his copses with tall arbours and trellises. The gardens, dotted with statues and looking towards the west, bore witness to the strictness of the King's ideas and to his insatiable will to make the world conform to the unwavering straight line of his dreams. By way of counterpoint, the pools and fountains currently under construction in the park would soon provide undulating new horizons. Before long France would have a palace worthy of its new greatness.

Far away from Versailles, the Abbé Strozzi spared no expense to lure to France, and above all to the King, the most eminent painters, sculptors and craftsmen. All over the world ambassadors, explorers, merchants and missionaries bore witness to the omnipotence of France and its Most Christian Monarch, who had just overcome the city of Ghent and reduced to silence the great marshals of Europe besieged behind its walls.

XII

Within the château, crowds swarmed through the corridors; outside in the grounds they flocked along the paths and around the ornamental pools and the kitchen garden. They were accompanying the King as he discovered and delighted in his new domain. Sometimes, in the afternoon, La Quintinie even came across courtiers who treated his garden as a convenient place for a stroll, some of them actually sprawling in the shade of his fruit trees. But so long as they didn't trample on his plants or bother him with silly questions, he had decided to accept them. He was glad his garden was so popular. To those of his staff who complained about the visitors he would say, "Our work feeds people's eyes as well as their stomachs. What more could we ask?"

→→←←

One morning the vegetables in several beds were found uprooted and, among the trees and espaliers, whole branches stripped of their fruit. Nothing else had been touched.

"We must tell the King!" cried La Quintinie's assistants angrily.

"Why?" he asked. "Just because someone's stolen a few apples and a couple of rows of onions? That would cause a lot of fuss over nothing. Come now, get on with your work and think no more about it."

Faced with his quiet authority, tempers cooled as fast as they had previously flared. But somehow news of the incident spread beyond the kitchen garden and the King intervened in person.

"Why did you not tell me of this pilfering, Monsieur de La Quintinie?" he said. "And who are these people who I'm told come and stroll around your garden every day?"

"Sire," answered La Quintinie, "I take the view that the theft took place on my territory, and I didn't think it worthwhile to trouble Your Majesty over a handful of stolen fruit. As for the people you mention —"

The King interrupted him. "You are mistaken, monsieur," he said. "Theft is theft and must be suitably punished. Moreover you seem to have forgotten that what you call your territory was mine in the first place. So pray, in future, be good enough to keep me informed of everything however trivial that happens in your garden, and be sure you deny access there to anyone who doesn't work for you or come there on my instructions."

Bontemps carried out a thorough investigation, questioning the gardener himself and his staff as well as people who'd been found disporting themselves in the kitchen garden. But of course no one had seen or heard anything. The King ordered guards to be posted.

La Quintinie went to him to object.

"Sire, my garden isn't a prison. Are we supposed to set snares for the birds and the insects too?"

The King was clearly annoyed and gave no answer. But luckily the guards were not too zealous, and it wasn't unusual for them to be found snoozing during the warmest part of the afternoon. And La Quintinie was glad to see that people had started strolling around the kitchen garden again.

One morning as he was watching his men picking tomatoes, La Quintinie was told that the thieves had been found. They were a couple of peasants who lived a few leagues away from Versailles and had been guilty of similar offences before. After close examination they had confessed and been summarily sentenced to twenty strokes of the rod.

La Quintinie hastened to see the King, but could not find him. A footman said he was in Le Nôtre's maze with some of his courtiers. The gardener hurried past the ornamental pool and turned into the box-lined labyrinth. From some way off, above the hedges, arose points of parasols, bursts of laughter, and cries of "Where are you? I can't see you!" The voices grew clearer and at last La Quintinie heard that of the King, together with others he did not recognise. But despite his efforts he couldn't find his way to the group. So he called to the King through the intervening hedges.

"Why such severity, Majesty? Why such a disparity between the crime these men committed and the punishment you mean to inflict on them?"

"Who's that?" asked a voice. "Answer."

"Jean-Baptiste de La Quintinie, gardener to His Majesty. Why are you set upon punishing these men so harshly, Sire?"

"Who are you talking about, monsieur?" demanded the King. "I don't understand."

"The people who robbed my garden a week ago."

There was no reply. Probably the King and his companions had turned into another path: inside the maze a few steps were enough to bring people much closer together or keep them much farther apart. La Quintinie tried to get his bearings. The sounds he could hear seemed to come from all directions at once. Where was the King? How could he get closer to him? All the paths looked alike. Then suddenly, as the gardener was about to give up and retrace his footsteps, the King's powerful voice came from behind a dense curtain of foliage. The gardener started. How had the King managed to find him?

"Where should we be, Monsieur de La Quintinie, if we did not deal harshly with such offences? We should only be encouraging other ravages, other thefts, each one greater than the last. "'Give them an inch . . .'"

"'And they'll take a yard.' I know, Your Majesty," answered La Quintinie, trying as he spoke to approach the source of the voice. "But if Your Majesty will allow me to give my opinion, I believe mercy on your part would have a more salutary effect on the people than sternness."

"Pray, Monsieur of the kitchen garden, keep your observations to yourself," thundered the invisible monarch.

"But —"

"Au revoir, monsieur."

And as La Quintinie struggled to find the way out of the labyrinth he heard the laughter start again and fill the whole garden.

→>-<←

A platform with two posts on it was put up at the entrance to the marble courtyard, and Canto read out the sentence to the sound of a long roll of drums.

La Quintinie had watched from a distance as the crowd gathered to wait for the victims to arrive. He had heard the cries that followed every volley of blows. He had prayed God to forgive both the King and the court. He also asked for mercy for himself, for not having been strong enough to prevent all this, for not having the courage to quit this world and this land of lies, the land he had spent years, a whole lifetime, creating but which nonetheless was not his.

XIII

With time, the tensions between the King and the gardener faded. In the weeks that followed their difference of opinion, the monarch, anxious to retain the services of a man whom so many envied him, did his best to be pleasant and considerate. He often referred to recent events, reproaching himself for his intransigence. In the course of a long walk in the direction of Marly, he also informed his gardener that he'd allocated him more money.

"Enough for you to enlarge your garden further and cultivate all the new species you like."

La Quintinie noticed the way the King emphasised the word "your". But he betrayed no sign of delight or gratitude.

"No," he thought while the King was still speaking, "the garden isn't mine. But what does it matter? We possess nothing in this world, or almost nothing. We ought not to fight against the things that are inevitable, but rather use them to fight against the things that can and must change. That's where our strength lies. And that's how we shall win our freedom."

The peasants around Versailles had never seen him put such energy into explaining his methods; into ordering cartloads of manure to be delivered to them when he didn't actually drive it there himself; into visiting them in their houses in the evening and reading aloud whole pages from Crescenzi's book on rural and agricultural improvement or the great Olivier de Serres' volume on farm management. For he had resolved to give these men and women all of what little he had. In order that their lives, and his own, should change at last.

+>-<+

"As my friend Primi Visconti so rightly says," Dancourt wrote to him one day, "'The court is probably the best comedy in the world.' Everything there is pretence and deception, even in church, where Madame de Montespan flaunts herself at the same time as Mademoiselle de Fontanges, the King's new favourite. The former sits with her children in the gallery on the left; the latter sits in the gallery on the right. Both pray ecstatically, shutting their eyes like saints at the elevation of the host, while the King sits there very pleased with himself at being able to take in both his mistresses at one glance. People sing the praises of Madame de Montespan's virtue; then they extol the other one's style. There's not a single woman here who doesn't long to have her hair dressed 'à la Fontanges'. As they say their prayers they all wish they could be like the first and look like the second.

"The news you send of your garden interests me greatly. Please go on telling me about it as long as you feel like it. It gives me pleasure to think there is one place in the world that's not part of this vast masquerade."

+>-<+

As he had promised in his last letter, Louis Morin arrived one cold rainy March morning in a coach laden with basins and bowls and strange, complicated-looking instruments.

"Monsieur de La Quintinie?" he inquired before even alighting. "I am happy to meet you at last. I have found your letters most

[66]

interesting. Forgive me for not answering all of them and for not dealing with every one of your questions – my research takes up nearly all my time. I am particularly drawn to the idea of helping you in your own work, the more so as I believe that people like you, who know so many of the secrets of our world, will be of valuable assistance to *me*. We have both made considerable progress, but there is still much work to do before we can make accurate long-term weather forecasts."

"And I am very glad to meet you," answered La Quintinie, surprised at so much magnanimity and so many words. "Would you like to rest for a while? I know the journey from Paris must have been tiring – I made it once myself."

"Thank you – no. I am anxious to begin my experiments as soon as possible. As soon as you have shown me my apartments and my servants have unloaded the coach, I'll start work."

As the two men walked southward through the garden, La Quintinie ventured to ask:

"How do you manage to predict the weather?"

"By observing what happens in the world, as you yourself do certainly better than I. The clouds, the moon, the leaves and the flowers. But observing such phenomena is not enough in itself for making long-term forecasts. And that's where we members of the Academy come in, with our highly developed instruments. In a little while I'll show you how they work. Our work consists of taking regular measurements and samples that we record in special notebooks, and from these we derive norms and variations."

"How far ahead can you foretell the weather?"

"One day in advance, for certain. Two days with a small margin of error. It depends on a number of parameters: the atmosphere is very unreliable."

The gardener pulled a face: he'd hoped Morin would be able to see farther ahead. The other seemed to divine his thoughts.

"Our science is in its infancy. But soon, very soon, I assure you, we'll be able to make much longer and more accurate forecasts."

For five days Morin emerged only briefly from his apartments, appearing just early in the morning or at nightfall. On these occasions he would be holding a small windpump, writing notes in big thick ledgers, muttering to himself, or planting balls of wool in the ground, impaled on wooden stakes. Sometimes the only thing to be seen of him all day was his arm sticking out of the window holding a glass tube that seemed to be collecting something. A candle burned in his room until far into the night. The whole garden was amused by the meteorologist's curious behaviour.

Finally, at the end of the fifth day, he came to see La Quintinie. He looked exhausted, and handed his host a sheet of paper on which the writing showed signs of lack of sleep.

"*Monday: Will be cold, with clear sky,*" it read. "*Tuesday: Still cold, with clear sky, but cloudy at the end of the day.*"

Without a word Morin turned and went back to his apartments. And on the following two days each forecast proved miraculously correct. La Quintinie was amazed not so much by this exploit as by the man responsible for it, living a lonely and arduous life himself in an attempt to improve the lives of others.

The weeks that followed were devoted to the gardener's apprenticeship. Morin taught him to use the instruments and pronounced him "extremely capable". He soon learned how to handle Torricelli's barometer and Huygens' thermometer; how to gauge the humidity of the air and measure the speed of the wind. To his new scientific observations he added his own knowledge of nature. When rain was imminent the balls of wool became heavier; dandelion and convolvulus flowers closed; the leaves on bean plants stood up. The weather improved for some time whenever the barometric pressure rose and the clouds that appeared at sunrise dispersed quickly. Late evening clouds tinged with yellow were a sign that it was going to be windy. And so, combining their knowledge and their love of the natural world, the two men succeeded in predicting the weather over a period of three days, without ever getting it wrong.

Soon all Versailles knew that the kitchen garden harboured two oracles. People crowded outside to consult them. The King himself questioned them before deciding whether to go riding or hunting.

Even after Morin had gone back to Paris people still came to ask La Quintinie's advice, and he was always willing to answer questions from monarch and courtier alike. One day the Comte de Namour presented himself.

"My dear La Quintinie, do you remember Madame and Monsieur d'Ardeville? Well, they are staying not far from Versailles at this moment. You can't have forgotten how eager they were to come to see you. Like many others they have heard a lot about your prophecies, and they propose to come to visit you the day after tomorrow. But they are worried because the weather has been so changeable for the last few days. Monsieur d'Ardeville doesn't know whether to come in his coach because the roof tends to fly off in the wind and Madame is anxious about her gown and her hair. So they have asked me to ask you what the weather is going to be like in two days' time."

"Two days from now? I think it will be sunny."

In the event, it rained hard, and the d'Ardevilles never did reach Versailles.

"What can you expect?" said La Quintinie to Namour. "Meteorology is in its infancy, and the atmosphere is very unreliable . . ."

For their part the peasants whom the gardener visited daily both admired and feared the little man who dabbled in the great mysteries of earth and heaven.

XIV

La Quintinie had seen a growing number of workmen slowly gathering round him. Just a few at first, drawn by curiosity and glad to have their feet on the ground again after hours perched on cranes or rickety scaffolding. Then during the few days that followed they would come back, bringing others with them.

It wasn't long before, as they gathered at nightfall amid the beds of marrows and tomatoes, they got talking about work, the many quarrels it generated and the even more frequent accidents. As they ate a bowl of soup or a plate of fried aubergines, they spoke of their homes far away and of their wives and children.

"My son will soon be three."

"My wife will soon be brought to bed. I've two boys already."

"I've got four. When I go home I'm going to teach them my trade."

They soon admitted that they weren't really up to writing to their families, and the public scribes who offered their services around the building sites asked exorbitant fees. So the gardener made time to help them. In a few simple words and in large, easily read characters he would transcribe the workaday stories, cheerful or sad, that they told him. For those whose loved ones couldn't read, he drew pictures. Sometimes, as a former lawyer, he would be consulted about a case of overdue compensation, and then he would write to Colbert or to the King.

Thus those other lives, recounted and committed to paper, became part of his own.

→—◄—

"So, my dear La Quintinie, are you satisfied with your new land?"

"I may say so, Sire. There were difficulties at first but now, by dint of work and perseverance, it is more manageable. A little while ago we planted the first strawberries in the enclosure near your own special entrance to the garden. And the fruit trees from your old garden seem very happy in the soil we prepared for them."

"They haven't suffered too much from being transplanted, then?"

"Not at all. I noticed a long time ago that when a tree is transplanted it gets its nourishment not from the small roots that haven't been taken away but from the new ones it grows after it has been moved. So I had my men cut off the rootlets, which hold the tree back rather than help it grow."

"How much longer will the work last?"

"It's difficult to predict exactly. At present only a few sections are producing crops. We may have to wait another two or three years before the garden bears all the fruit and vegetables it's capable of. And many of the new arrangements have yet to be put into practice. Monsieur Hardouin-Mansart still hasn't even finished the plans for the pool in the Grand Carré."

"I'll look into the matter. Speaking of new arrangements, I have some good news for you. Monsieur Fordrin tells me he's nearly finished the gate I shall use in future when I come to visit you. It's a magnificent piece of work. But" – and here the King smiled – "many of us think its beauty is not to be compared with that of your own work. So we have decided to increase your emoluments. From now on you will receive eighteen thousand livres a year. Naturally you will be responsible for paying your men and your casual labourers and for the upkeep of your equipment."

La Quintinie was less elated by the increase in his funds than by the fact that the King and his courtiers were taking such an interest in his work. He kept in mind the King's autocratic attitude to his subjects and the society he claimed to rule. But he did say to himself, "After all, how can the rest of us understand the destiny of such a man?"

→>—<←

"Can you be made docile and forgetful just by a flattering word and a little money?" Neuville objected. "You are grateful to the King for acknowledging your merits. Who could have failed to recognise them? You tell me about the money. It's only fair you should have more. I must admit I find your last letter very upsetting."

"What can I do, Philippe? Yes, I am glad to think that the King appreciates my work. But I'm even happier to think that because of his liberality I'll be able to help the poor people who live near my garden and have such great need of my researches. I want to do all I can now to change their lives for the better."

"I fear you may be lowering yourself and expending a lot of energy for nothing," replied Neuville bluntly. "How many of them really want their lives changed? People often equate change with improvement. Just give your peasants and workmen a bit more money or a bit more land, make them a few promises, and you'll hear no more complaints. It's no use wanting to change people's lives if they won't change themselves first."

Neuville was probably right. What could he, a humble gardener, do for all these folk made fearful and submissive by poverty, apart from handing out encouraging words, cartloads of manure and the occasional bowl of soup?

"These men have turned my life upside down, and by that I don't just mean I am moved by their fate. Perhaps I shall never be able to change their lives profoundly. But if I can't transform the people themselves at least I can go on trying to improve their land and cure their ills. I like to think that when they have enough to survive on, then they may start to think about living."

→>-<-

Not far from his apartments La Quintinie had marked out a special plot of fertile soil where he opened up pleasant-smelling trenches; where he harrowed, dressed and rolled, heaped up ridges and banks, and finally sowed flowers and vegetables. In this open-air laboratory every plant was given constant attention. The gardener introduced new techniques of propagation – using cuttings and layering. He grafted, trained and staked some species, rounded out the foliage of others, used all his skill to develop his plants' resistance to bad weather. His seed-beds inter-mingled different kinds of plants for mutual support: tomatoes went perfectly with lettuces and cabbages; parsley with carrots; carrots with cauliflowers. To repel slugs and snails he planted thyme and sage; ants were discouraged by elder and nasturtiums, flies by basil, honey bees by the flowers of comice pears, mice and voles by spurge, onions and a kind of clover.

The gardener also studied the various possible uses and applications of his plants. He read Paracelsus's *Herbarium* and the *Antidotarium Florentinum* and followed their teachings. Thus carrots, eaten raw, were good for sluggish digestions; cooked, they cured diarrhoea. Wild pansies were used to treat rheumatism and skin diseases. Cabbage leaves cauterised unhealed wounds; burdock, hyssop and figwort soothed the wheezing coughs common in the muddy lands of the west; aubergines, asparagus and onions had diuretic properties; pumpkin seeds acted as a vermifuge.

One room in the gardener's apartments had been converted into an apothecary's shop, where the books bearing the names of the most eminent *patres farmacognosiae* mingled with a wide variety of instruments: Albertus Magnus, Nicolas Monardes, Pierandrea Mattioli, Andreas Libavius and Otto Brunfels rubbed shoulders with mortars, scales, cauldrons, albarello, bottles of tinctures. La Quintinie often worked late preparing his concoctions.

The little experimental plot became his main object in life. As for the larger garden around his tiny empire, he handed it over for the time being to his best-qualified assistants. For their part, they had begun to be concerned about their master's state of mind.

XV

 In March 1679 people began worrying about poisoning again. It was said that a witch had been arrested – a former midwife known as La Voisin who had been visited in her own home by many men and women of high degree. She had supplied them with philtres, unguents and "inheritance powders". It was also said that a number of courtiers were involved in peculiar affairs concerning black masses and child murder. It was even alleged that the lives of the King, the Dauphin and Colbert had been in danger. Members of the court had taken to once more shutting themselves up in their apartments and treating their neighbours with suspicion.

Some temporary reassurance was provided by the convocation of a *Chambre ardente*. This was a special tribunal initiated in the sixteenth century for dealing with serious crimes like heresy, devil-worship and poisoning, and called "the burning chamber" because its black draperies were lit by candles day and night. As a result of La Voisin's revelations La Reynie made many arrests, a number of which caused great surprise. But soon a different kind of apprehension arose. It was rumoured that Louis Boucherat, president of the *Chambre ardente*, might declare sodomy to be a crime. Many courtiers began to fear that they might spend the rest of their lives in prison.

→>-<←

One morning La Quintinie received alarming tidings from Neuville.

"Did you know," he wrote, "that Dancourt has been in prison for over a month? La Voisin is said to have incriminated him when she was being questioned. I've made several attempts to visit him in his cell, but I've always been refused entrance. As a result of my persistence I've even come under suspicion myself."

Was this what Dancourt had been hinting at when he talked of turning the world upside down? It was all scarcely credible.

"I'm told our friend is in reasonable health," Neuville went on. "His gaolers are well-disposed and let food through to him from outside without so much as touching it. I'm convinced he is innocent. It's only to be hoped he will soon be set free."

→>-<+

Bontemps and his "blue boys" turned up one day at the gates to the garden, and after carrying out a thorough search of La Quintinie's apartments emerged with a bundle of letters. La Quintinie was summoned to the palace, but freed a couple of hours later.

"But kindly hold yourself at our disposal for a while, and see to it that any plants in your garden that might be used in the making of poison are destroyed," Bontemps had concluded.

So they had to uproot from the little garden whole beds of barberries, birchwort, aconites, colchicum, vetch, belladonna, fumitory and bois-jolis that the gardener had patiently coaxed to maturity.

→>-<+

Months went by. The poisons scandal hung fire, but Dancourt did not reappear. Neuville had finally lost track of him.

"I've been everywhere – to the Bastille, the Petit Châtelet, Fort-l'Evêque. I even went to the Salpêtrière. But no one could tell me anything. Has he been freed? Have you had any news?"

La Quintinie knew nothing, of course. Dancourt had vanished, lock, stock and barrel – "and that barrel would be the last straw for a man like him," commented Namour, who was soon able to boast that his jest was on everyone's lips.

More months went by before the gardener learned what had really happened. Dancourt had been found hanged in his cell in August. Some people believed it was suicide and that this desperate act was proof of guilt. But not long afterwards, in the course of the police's investigations, a man called Doncour was arrested and admitted to dealings with the famous La Voisin. He was swiftly executed. Dancourt's death was hushed up, and his body hastily thrown into a common grave.

"I feel his tragic end as much as you do," Neuville wrote to La Quintinie. "But at least those who pass on bring those who remain closer together. Believe me, more than ever your friend."

→>-<←

"Why do you insist on forcing everything into a definite form?" Neuville asked one day. "I've just been looking at the drawings you sent me of your fruit trees: the branches are fixed to the walls in such a way that they'll soon completely cover them. Perhaps you'll think I'm being unduly severe again. But why must you torture your trees in the same way as Monsieur Le Nôtre ill-treats his gardens? Didn't your old fruit trees produce a good crop when you left them alone? Isn't the world beautiful in itself without our having to interfere so tyrannically? I admit it's man's duty to help the world bring forth, but not to control and constrain it in the way you speak of and demonstrate. I hold that trees set out in rows and clipped into artificial shapes become fragile. If we want things to last we must combine pragmatism and chance."

"Not only does growing fruit on espaliers make the trees more productive," replied the gardener, "it also gives me the pleasure of hoping that one day nature will have covered the walls entirely. In summer the stone will be all vegetation, and in winter the vegetation will be all stone. I like to think that in uniting the two I am creating a new universe in which time passes more slowly and there is less loneliness. An enclosed world, yet one without boundaries. A new country, hitherto unknown, where it will be agreeable to think and walk and live. I heard recently that someone called Edmé Mariotte has described how plants derive nourishment from the earth and the air. Do you know the book or its title? No one here can tell me anything about it. I often think about Dancourt. Yesterday I planted a pear tree, a Bon-Chrétien, in memory of him. I put it in a separate bed and I shall leave it free to spread its branches as it likes. I do hope I'll see you soon. My men and my trees hear so much about you."

→><+<

It would soon be October. The first frosts had to be countered by lighting fires near the vegetable beds in the evening; the heavy smoke from the resin acted as protection. The more fragile plants had to be sheltered under glass or in frames. Matting must be fixed over the espaliers. Canvas shields had to be put round the trees at dusk; cucumbers and melons needed to be earthed up. The manure in the seed-beds had to be constantly renewed. It was tiring work. But La Quintinie liked being the first to arrive in his garden on those chill misty mornings. A nearby bell would sound the dawn Angelus, and from outside the high walls he could hear the peasants calling out to one another, the lowing of oxen and the echo of ploughshares striking the frozen earth. The crystal-clear air made all these sounds ring out over the surrounding forests and hills. Then slowly all fell silent. The day labourers appeared at last, drowsy or shouting and bawling, their teeth chattering or clapping their hands together against the cold. But in a while, after they'd set about their work, their woollen cloaks were no longer needed and would be thrown aside onto a fence or over the fork of a tree.

Every morning the garden presented the same unchanging order.

→>–<←

"Forgive this long silence, my dear Jean-Baptiste: the last few months have been occupied with new and worrying business. Did you know that last July the mixed courts consisting of equal numbers of Catholics and Protestants were abolished without warning? So now the Protestants have no legal safeguards. I have been busy writing a number of articles on the subject: one of them appeared in the *Mercure galant* a few weeks ago. It was by no means plain sailing: Jean Donneau de Vizé and Thomas Corneille, the editors, were very apprehensive. Fortunately Monsieur Fontenelle intervened and took my side. He's a strange character, but delightful company. I'll introduce you to him one day.

"Port-Royal, the 'dreadful valley', as Madame de Sévigné calls it, was dissolved in November. The King, it seems, 'dislikes anything that makes a noise'. Or so says Harlay de Champvallon, the Archbishop of Paris. And what about the noise of the King's artillery? No, with all due respect to Champvallon, it isn't noise the King's afraid of. It's murmurs. And the gentlemen of Port-

Royal, as they are called, have got into the habit of murmuring too often for his taste against him and the people who make God say what they themselves want to hear. The King 'dislikes anything that makes a noise' – but he's going to hear plenty of noise, I assure you. There are many of us, in France and elsewhere, who condemn this spiritual repression. I've started working on my pamphlet again and add to it every day. I shan't rest until I've finished it and had it published.

"Yes, I'd like to pay you a visit and show your trees my face at last – the face of him you've told them so much about. But recent events have caused me some anxiety, and I fear that if I came I might bring trouble on you too. But I don't despair of seeing you again one day. When the weather is better for both of us, perhaps. Meanwhile my thoughts are with you.

"Mariotte published the results of his observations in a book called *A Treatise on the Growth of Plants*. Let me know if you can't get a copy and I'll try to send you one from Paris."

→>-<+

There were more and more accidents, including fatal ones, on the building sites at Versailles, and also at Marly, where they were shifting quantities of earth to install a huge hydraulic machine designed by a Walloon engineer called Rennequin Sualem. Compensation for the victims of these mishaps was slow to materialise and there had been rumblings of revolt, swiftly suppressed by the police.

Then a new kind of person was to be seen in the corridors and in the immediate vicinity of the château: men with only one arm or leg or who had lost an eye; others were consumptive. All were waiting to be paid forty, sixty or a hundred livres, according to the extent of their injury. The King ordered them to be removed. Some were put in makeshift barracks at a distance from the château. Those who were in a really bad way were sent to the General Hospital in Paris, where they slowly finished dying, forgotten by all.

→>-<-

One morning as the monarch and his architects were inspecting the progress of the various building works, a haggard-looking woman, her bosom bare, burst from the crowd and ran towards the King. She was restrained none too gently by two guards.

"Tyrant! Machine-worshipper!" she cried, struggling to be freed. "My son was killed yesterday falling off some scaffolding. What for? What for? What do we get out of all this folly of yours? Nothing but death!"

"Are you speaking to me?" asked the King, obviously surprised.

"Who else, whoremonger of a King?" she shouted wildly.

With a wave of the hand the King sentenced her to be flogged.

"I happened to witness the scene yesterday, as I was on my way to fetch water," wrote the gardener. "The worst thing about it, Philippe, was that no one lifted a finger. The workers stood there speechless, their arms hanging at their sides. But what else could they do? Not a single courtier dared to oppose the King's will. As for me, I didn't like to interfere. I don't know what to do any more . . .

"The hospitals here are appalling – full of grey faces, blank looks, failing bodies, shouting and shame. Versailles has turned into a dreadful battlefield.

"This morning I went for a walk up on Satory Hill. For the first time. The sky was grey and silent. One really ought to look at Versailles from up there. It's like some gigantic ant-hill, a vast confused mass of men, materials and sounds. I came to a little ruined chapel at the top of the hill, and despite the danger from falling masonry I went inside. The light there was dim and pleasant. Part of the ceiling had fallen in and the chapel was open to the sky. I found another door and went through it. Suddenly there lay before me a great expanse of virgin earth and sky. I could see nothing but patches of heather and broom entangled in wind and light. For hours I followed a winding path made by wild animals, through an empty world under mountainous clouds echoing to the cries of solitary birds. I forgot all about the human race."

XVI

At the end of 1679, despite exceptionally severe weather, the King came to Versailles very often. He was seen going more and more frequently in the direction of Marly, together with a small group of chosen companions. It soon became known that he had given Mansart a new task there – to build a new château into which he could withdraw from the world whenever he felt like it. What! was the King already contemplating going elsewhere before his enormous palace at Versailles was even finished? It was incomprehensible. Many people thought the pious Madame de Maintenon was behind the new building project. Going to Marly, they jested, was tantamount to going into a hermitage. Hadn't he, in the last few months, been seen more and more often at church at ten in the morning, soberly dressed, carrying a rosary, and chanting the *Domina salvum fac Regem* with eyes half-shut after the last Gospel reading? Everyone else now began to be concerned about their salvation. The chapels had never seen such congregations. The courtiers flocked there, preceded the evening before by flunkeys wearing ribbons or red velvet badges to identify their employers; they sometimes came to blows in their efforts to secure good seats for their masters. People came to church eagerly to hear long and lurid sermons, drinking in disturbing paradoxes and peremptory assertions with equal satisfaction. When preachers like Bossuet, Harlay de Champvallon or Le

Tellier came to Versailles they played to packed congregations.

"Everyone now copies the King and his mistress and pretends to be very pious. The people you tell me about make me laugh, Jean-Baptiste. I come across the same sort myself in Notre-Dame and other Paris churches. If I'm not mistaken, the chapel at Versailles is quite near the theatre. How apt! I am afraid that most people go to one place imagining they're in the other! Before appearing before God they think about how they appear before men. They fidget, they chat, they flaunt themselves – sometimes they even fight. Finally they emerge, eyes and hearts and brains all damp and tearful if the preacher happened to speak well, dry as a bone if he expressed himself badly. But what about their souls? Where do they come in? Very likely they don't come in at all amid this agitation of the senses. These people want to save their souls, but all they think about is protecting their bodies, their fortunes and their status against the decay to come. What we fear most is not God so much as the insects, the stones and the black earth whose prisoners we shall be until the Last Judgment. What can God do with all these shams? Ever since we placed man in the centre of the universe we banished God from it. He's probably waiting somewhere out there beyond the unmoving stars for us to finish ourselves off at last so that He can create the universe all over again."

"No, Philippe – God isn't all that far away from us. It may even be He's so close that we can no longer see Him. But He's there, to be sure, between the branches at night, under the moss, inside the trunks of trees, in the heart of stones and among the clouds. God cares nothing for the gilt and marble in which men think to worship Him. Don't look for Him in the churches, Philippe. He long ago took his leave of them through a side door opening onto the world."

XVII

To begin with it was just a faint gleam visible in the sky near Orion on moonless nights. Then gradually it shone more brightly and could be seen on cloudy nights and sometimes in the daytime. What was this glittering shape growing ever larger in the sky and in men's minds? Everyone was lost in conjecture and all the telescopes in Paris were trained on the heavens.

→>-<←

So many conflicting theories reached Versailles about this phenomenon that different parties formed. Some took a scientific point of view and talked of the "combustion" of a star. Those of a mystical persuasion saw it as "God's Chariot visiting the King". Others interpreted the incandescent sphere as a portent of the end of the world. The debates were so heated that the participants would often resort to fisticuffs.

Finally came the news that an Englishman, Edmund Halley, had explained the mystery. It was a comet, an immense boulder that had been hurtling through space for countless ages. Apparently, said the astronomer, it had decided to end its journey on earth, where the impact would be so great that the whole planet would explode. Everyone was terrified. The courtiers forgot their quarrels and their poisons. Parquet floors seemed to shake, fountains to go dry. What mistake had they made, what sin had they committed, to deserve such punishment? People flocked anew to church. Paray-le-Monial resounded with the chanting and prayers of pilgrims. The ball in the sky went on growing. People gave alms to the poor. The King tried to demonstrate his super-natural powers by "touching" hundreds of people suffering from scrofula. The sky was aflame. People lay low, got drunk; some ran away. The end of the world.

One morning a horde of flea-ridden prophets with fiery gestures and mad eyes appeared from no one knew where, making women swoon and stouter spirits fall to their knees. "Huge hailstones started to pelt down on men from the heavens, and men cursed God because of this terrible scourge!" they cried, echoing the words of St John the Divine. The intruders were arrested or driven away, but they returned next day in even greater numbers and addressed the crowd from walls or make-shift platforms: "Alas! Alas! This great city, that was clothed in fine linen and purple and scarlet and decked with gold and pearls and precious stones – how is it that such wealth has vanished in the twinkling of an eye? Beseech God, the principal of all things, for mercy. Beware of the lake of fire and sulphur, the second death."

One of the strangers in particular attracted attention. He spoke rarely and seldom moved, but his silence, his looks and his enor-mous moustache were intriguing. No one knew who he was or where he came from, but that didn't matter. The people crowded round him, waiting for a word or a gesture. At last the prophet spoke. He did not mention God or the Apocalypse; only stars and interplanetary journeys. He said he had travelled through the universe on a moonbeam, visiting the whole of space before falling down to earth. In the course of his long voyage he had met strange nations. He numbered Saturnines, Martians, Mercurians and Selenites among his friends. They had charged him with the task of explaining the sign in the heavens to the inhabitants of the earth. It was a sign not of the end of time, but of a new time, a new era.

"The King will die," he said. "And dark days will follow, bringing disease, famine and unrest. But a few of the most righteous men will survive the great cataclysm."

But what were people to do to deserve to go on living? Though they showered him with sumptuous presents the soothsayer refused to answer that question.

"The time is not yet come," was all he would say.

→>−<←

To everyone's astonishment the gardener seemed unaffected by the growing panic. No one ever saw him mingling with the crowd to consult the oracles. Had the fumes from his reeking soil turned his brain and divorced him from reality? Or had his daily observations of the sky brought him closer than anyone else to the truth? The crowd pursued him even to his garden.

"Do you know something?" they asked. "Tell us, we implore you!"

But La Quintinie said nothing. Through the gaunt branches of his apple trees he merely looked on at the vain agitation of men and women who had never thought that one day they would die, and who had simply forgotten to live.

→>−<←

"The churches in Paris are full," wrote Neuville. "The priests aren't content with celebrating two or three masses a day in different places. Yesterday there were ten communion services at Notre-Dame alone. It's a question now not only of appearing but of appearing to appear. But I can't help smiling when I see these people presenting themselves before God dressed up in their superstitions. Some come with their pockets full of olive branches that have been steeped for three days in glasses of well water. Others keep their mouths wide open during the *elevatio*, or clutch in their hand a parchment with the *Sanctus* written on it. All this to persuade God to spare them. And the priests approve such antics. Sometimes they even bless animals brought to them for the purpose. What a tragi-comedy!

"Not a morning goes by without people discovering fresh suicides," he went on. "The corpses are found hanging by a rope, or with their bodies covered in purple marks, or with a bullet in the head. Sometimes singly; sometimes in groups. A whole family committed suicide yesterday. The father cut the throats of his wife and children and then held a pistol to his own head. How is it possible for people to kill themselves because they're afraid of death? It can only be cowardice or pride. Not courage! A coward runs away into death to escape the awfulness of what remains of his life. A proud man thinks himself the master of his fate right down to the choice of his own death. But while a brave man knows very well how parlous his situation is, he just accepts it. He is the 'thinking reed' that Pascal speaks of, who may sway in a storm but who stands firm, awaiting his last hour with confidence, having come to terms with his life and adjusted to his death, and at peace with the God he has chosen for himself.

"'To everything there is a season,'" says Ecclesiastes, "'and a time to every purpose under the heaven. A time to be born, and a time to die; a time to plant, and a time to pluck up that which is planted.'"

->-<-

The comet went away, and people's apprehensions with it. The prophets disappeared too. Everyone returned to their usual activities and laughed at their earlier fears. Death had passed them by.

→>-<-

La Quintinie resumed his work in a calmer atmosphere. The days were all the same. Time seemed to stand still, stuck in the repetition of trivial tasks and the recurrence of trivial anxieties. What was the use of raking and hoeing, of worrying about whether fruit and vegetables would reach maturity safely? His memory was full of the blazing trail of the comet. Beside that, everything seemed pointless and ridiculous. What was human life, he thought, but a race that had to be run over and over again, a meaningless struggle to establish the greatness of a King or a God? And would he himself ever change anything in the lives of the peasants and workmen who were still suffering and dying around him?

Day after day, astride the furrows in his garden, he waited. He was waiting for something stronger than the wind or the rain – something enormous that would put an end to these shapeless, colourless days and allow his life to collapse once and for all.

XVIII

"The Intendant of Poitiers, a certain René de Marillac, has launched what he euphemistically calls 'missionaries in boots' against the Protestants of Poitou province. In fact they are soldiers, dragoons armed to the teeth and under orders to convert anyone who doesn't recognise the religion of the King. I have spent much time writing in the newspapers against these new severities and condemning them in public. I have met with friends who are fiercely, even violently, opposed to these measures. And yet ... Do you remember the letter in which I said that writing articles had given meaning to my life? How wrong I was! What is the use of holding forth and pointing out the inconsistencies between this and that while men are dying on their own land in defence of their liberty? What good does it do to argue about the truth when truth is absent from the hearts and souls of those who talk about it? There's no time to be lost now, Jean-Baptiste. I don't want to talk about anything from now on but what I have experienced myself. I've thought about it for a long time. I leave tomorrow for Niort with a few companions. No doubt I shan't change the course of history. But when I denounce suffering and intolerance it will no longer be empty words. Every syllable will be charged with what I have seen and felt. So perhaps what I say will in its turn manage to touch the hearts of those who read or hear them. I shall be thinking of you all the time."

The gardener was very alarmed by Neuville's letter. This sudden departure made him fear the worst. What would become of his friend, swept away in the current of a war not his own? And above all, might he not be making a mistake? Who would be willing to listen to him when he returned from his present expedition? La Quintinie could hear the courtiers, just like the labourers, approving of the King's religious policy as they strolled by outside the garden wall.

"My dear fellow, it's about time we brought those heretics to heel!"

"Absolutely. I was in Paris yesterday and I heard some very disturbing news while I was there. The heretics in Poitou are apparently taking up arms, setting fire to their villages and then making off to the woods and the marshes. They attack the missionaries day and night with unimaginable ferocity. If the army relaxes its vigilance for a moment all will be lost. But by the grace of Almighty God and of our omnipotent King, our men are well trained and armed to the hilt."

"Indeed. Thanks be to God and the King."

La Quintinie regretted that his friend had not written to him sooner. They might then have talked and exchanged points of view. Perhaps he could have made Neuville see the vanity of his struggle. Still, he couldn't help admiring him for accepting so unconditionally the course of action his fate laid upon him.

Neuville's zeal gradually revived the gardener's own courage, and he copied a quotation from Marcus Aurelius into his journal: "I shall do that which I was born to do." And what La Quintinie was born to do was to feed his fellow men, to provide them with the best of what nature had so patiently given him.

So he set to work again more feverishly than ever. From morn till night he and his assistants toiled away, digging, trimming, storing fruit and vegetables, weeding. Sometimes he would vanish for days at a time, visiting the peasants with his pockets full of seeds or books. He could also be seen in the crowded corridors of nearby hospitals, tending and comforting the sick. He didn't want to think any more; thinking no longer served any purpose. Giving and giving again to the limits of his strength, that was what he had to do. He would come back in the evening weary and stiff from his efforts, but he still found the energy to note down the results of the day's observations and experiments. When at last he blew out his candle he would sleep until dawn.

→>—<←

"We reached Niort without let or hindrance," wrote Neuville, "apart from being stopped and checked briefly once or twice on the way. The town looks as if it were under siege, with armed men everywhere and nothing to be heard but the thud of boots and the rattling of sabres. But we pressed on without difficulty across country to Mougon, where I have been for three days now. I hear some of the neighbouring villages have been ransacked and set on fire, and many of the people, men and women, tortured. Everyone is frantic with fear though they try not to show it. Those that are left are mostly peasants; the better-off fled to Holland or England a long time ago. The army is expected to arrive at any minute, but the people are wonderfully calm.

"Night fell a couple of hours ago but there isn't a star in the sky. I can see gleams of light on the hill opposite. Burning houses? Campfires? We are all waiting. It's as if time and space had suddenly closed in on us."

→>—<←

Summer came suddenly in the middle of May. An arid wind raised clouds of dust which got into eyes, ears and noses. The gardeners spent all their time protecting pots from the heat, spreading cloths over the more vulnerable seed-beds, watering the plants two or three times a day. La Quintinie spared no effort. He was especially concerned about his espaliers. Superfluous branches and leaves had to be carefully removed and the remainder trained along and fixed to the supporting walls. Not until the blazing sun had moved on from those walls could watering and lighter spraying begin. Trees had to be irrigated according to the direction in which they faced. Exposed stems and branches must be protected with a layer of lime mixed with clay. The only thing the workers stopped for was to slake their own thirst.

Some courtiers were in the habit of coming to tell La Quintinie about the latest happenings at court. But what was it to him if Mademoiselle de Fontanges had died in strange circumstances last June at Port-Royal? Or if new edicts had been issued allowing Protestant children to be converted at the age of seven? Or if the King had annexed Strasbourg to France? While the courtiers were talking excitedly about such things, the gardener was thinking how his fruit and vegetables made their way through people's insides, and picturing the slow transformation of matter as it combined with the humours to move the arms, legs and lips and animate the souls of the people who stood before him.

-->-<--

At last, after long weeks of silence, Neuville wrote again. Together with some of the local inhabitants he had had to flee Mougon when the dragoons threatened to lay siege to the town. The group had lain low for days in the surrounding woods, living like animals on such food and water as they could find. Then they had found refuge in a farm. Neuville preferred not to say where it was.

"If you could see the courage of these men and women!" he wrote. "They have lost everything – everything. But they never utter a word of complaint. They don't even wish for revenge. They just pray. I myself have no regrets. For now, among these people who confidently accept the possibility of their own deaths, I am at last beginning to live. I hope this letter reaches you safely."

→>–<←

The King sent La Quintinie a note from Fontainebleau:

"Our mind is made up and we have decided on the date of our forthcoming move to Versailles. It is to take place next May, though I shall ask you to keep this news to yourself for the time being. I should like to celebrate our arrival suitably, so shall ask you to see that your fruit and vegetable houses are ready to provide for the five thousand people who are to attend the ceremonies. Many of us admire your labours, my dear La Quintinie, and want to prove it to you. So this time pray grant us the pleasure of having you with us for supper without finding you have suddenly disappeared – an exploit you have shown a certain talent for hitherto. I long to see you again, and my Versailles, and my gardens and sky."

There was no news from Neuville.

XIX

The bearer of the letter had travelled across country, passed the outer and inner walls of the garden and searched along the box-lined paths for the gardener among his branches and furrows. Now La Quintinie held the envelope in his hand. His earth-stained fingers were trembling: he could see it was Neuville's handwriting.

"By some incomprehensible miracle we escaped. Suddenly one November morning Marillac's troops disappeared. We found out later that they'd been sent to Bayonne. Most of the people here see it as a gift from heaven. I don't know. So many things have happened since I last wrote to you. If you knew what I've seen ... But we escaped. I'm going back to Paris. I'm returning to let people know what these days and nights of terror have been like. To denounce the crimes that are committed in the name of a God with the face and the ways of a Bourbon. To tell of the courage of these men and women, and of the terrible gentleness in their eyes and in their actions.

"I believe I know men better now – I have a better under-standing of what they are and what they do. Recent events have convinced me of this: for too long we have banished from our minds the truth of our own death. But our instincts remember it, and so does our flesh, which knows it is conditioned by its own inevitable decay. So the body shouts and runs about and clings to other bodies, caressing some, repulsing others, loving them or hating them. But let the thought of death come to mind for a moment and the body falls silent, the lips close, and arms and legs all falter. And lo and behold, here comes the humble soul, together with the power of God, to save man from the abyss into which he was about to fall. But we should always hold on to the taste of that fear and remember the savour of our soul. We ought never to forget anything. But we do forget everything. And we forget ourselves all the time.

"I shall write it all down, Jean-Baptiste. I shall write it all down now because these recent weeks have taught me not to speak. I shall write to remind myself of those terrible days, to keep myself awake and alert in the midst of this world devoid of memory. And perhaps in the end I'll manage to awaken others. I like to think so."

So Philippe was coming back. The sky was opening up at last, and with it the future.

XX

'The King moved to Versailles last Wednesday. Someone came and told me about his spectacular arrival, with coaches, white horses and bays, musketeers, lines of Swiss and French guards. Everywhere you looked there were crowds shouting and cheering amid an uproar of trumpets and drums. But if you could see the château itself, Philippe, you wouldn't give three louis for it. Nothing is finished. Where the gardens should be there are open trenches for the most part and stretches of mud. The building itself is still in terrible chaos. In some places the roof, in others a whole floor is missing. I'm told the corridors are in an even more parlous state – full of masons, carpenters and decorators, together with all the dust they raise. The weather is very cold for May; the chimneys in the apartments smoke, when they don't actually catch fire! There are draughts everywhere. But nobody complains. Everyone puts a good face on it and professes to be delighted with the cramped, low-ceilinged quarters the King has handed out. Despite the cold they stroll around dear old Le Nôtre's cubes and curves, rhapsodising about his achievements. But as soon as they can they hurry back for a cup of hot chocolate or coffee in some little closet reeking with smoke.

"Work is especially difficult just now. The usual May frosts are early this year, and many of the fruit trees have suffered in spite of all our precautions. The water freezes in the irrigation channels, and it will probably be a long time before the fountain is working. But I think of you and your arrival, which I hope will be soon, and which will bring so much warmth and strength. I've heard nothing since you told me of your return. Do let me have news of you as quickly as you can."

→>-<-

By the end of the afternoon the first guests had already gathered in the marble courtyard around a buffet in the shape of a giant pyramid, laden with fruits, vegetables and different kinds of meat. A few days earlier the weather had suddenly turned milder, and that morning the King had announced that the banquet was to take place out of doors. Bows, curtseys and manly handshakes were to be seen on all sides. Military gentlemen, buoyed up in the pride of their recent victories, ogled ladies feeling more than usually susceptible. Servants carrying fine wines and elaborate petits fours had to elbow their way through a growing throng. At dusk the King, surrounded by his family, made a brief appearance on his balcony, to cheers from hundreds of courtiers and footmen. Torches were lit, and the fountains were illuminated by thousands of candles.

La Quintinie arrived late. The crowd was now vast, reminding him of the evening he had spent at the Louvre. As he approached he could make out little groups of men and women talking and laughing together, their mouths wide open.

Before the gardener had time to join the first of those walls of human flesh surmounted by wigs, Namour hurried up to him.

"Hallo, La Quintinie! I've been watching out for you for over an hour. The King is asking for you. Come this way and make haste — we should have been with him before now."

La Quintinie often thought he had lost his guide as the two of them made their way through the crowd. What could they all be talking about? He did catch snatches of conversation, but soon left them behind as he hurried by. He also left behind the whole sumptuously dressed crowd, gathered round a great mound of food laid out beneath the newly painted windows of their King.

The corridors of the palace were deserted. From beyond the windows came the sound of shouting and laughter mingled with the murmur of fountains playing and the sighing of the wind in the treetops. The two men went down more corridors littered with scaffolding, statues, lamps and chests of drawers. The noise from outside gradually abated. The walls were covered with gilt and colour, huge battle scenes from which emerged the armoured body and resolute countenance of the King.

At last they came to a heavy door inlaid with bronze, which was immediately thrown open by two guards. Then, in the flickering gold light of the chandeliers, La Quintinie saw a mass of men and women sitting laughing and drinking at a vast curved table.

"Well, well, Monsieur le jardinier," cried the King. "You almost kept us waiting!"

Everyone turned to look at La Quintinie, who felt himself blushing. He stammered an apology as best he could.

→>⋅<⋅

As a supreme honour, a chair with arm-rests had been kept for him on the King's right hand. The conversation in the early part of the evening was very pleasant. They spoke of fruit and how to ripen and store it, of fertilisers and the dangers of bad weather. The King put forward some discerning ideas on horticulture that showed how knowledgeable he was on the subject. As the King spoke, the gardener studied the great dignitaries of France assembled around him, the grand and wealthy personages who would consume the simple treasures he himself had spent months and years extracting from his land.

→>-<←

La Quintinie heard doors half opened and noticed anxious looks on footmen's faces. The food was about to arrive. His labour would soon be providing men with food. The King's twenty-four violinists played a composition by Lully, a voice cried, "Messieurs, to the King's table!" and the first salvers emerged from the antechambers.

Then walking solemnly towards him he saw the maître d'hotel, bearing a heavy staff, followed by an usher of the table carrying a torch, himself followed by the gentleman of the first dish, who preceded the gentleman of the second dish and the officers of the table carrying still more trays and dishes.

"What a lot of men, and what a lot of dishes!" thought the gardener, while the Grand Chamberlain named each dish as it passed before him.

"Asparagus broth *en vermeil*. Preserved artichokes in white sauce. Lentil soup *à l'huile*. Almond soup garnished with almonds *à la praline*. Mutton *au jus et à l'ail*. Ragout of roots and potherbs *à l'huile*. Oysters. Apricot horns *à la crème* . . ."

The gardener turned to Namour.

"We'll never be able to eat all that!"

"Probably not. But don't worry: the food won't be wasted. The officers of the table, who will clear it in due course, will share some of the leftovers between them and sell the rest. Have you ever noticed a terrace by the side of the rue de la Chancellerie, to the left of the parade ground?"

"Yes."

"That's where they take the remains of the dinners and suppers and sell them off cheap."

The King signalled to the Grand Chamberlain, who turned to the officers of the table and said:

"Messieurs, to the King's meat!"

A crowd of footmen swarmed round the table. Namour told La Quintinie their names and duties.

"That's the cup-bearer, who has to give the King something to drink whenever he asks for it. That's the head of the pantry. That's the head of the larder. I expect you recognise the lieutenant de fruiterie and the verdurier, to whom you deliver the fruit and vegetables."

Finally all the plates had been set out and everyone began to eat.

+>-<+

Towards the end of the supper the King turned, smiling radiantly, to his gardener.

"You're an artist, La Quintinie!" he said.

Yes, his labour had provided food for men. But how? He had scarcely recognised the vegetables that had been paraded before him. Some were cold, some drowned in thick sauces, or covered with complicated meats and champagne. He had seen the King stop bothering with his fork and swallow without ceremony two dozen oysters, a plateful of salad, some mutton, a plateful of pastries, and then some more fruit and a few hard-boiled eggs. Worse still, had he not seen him and some of his courtiers secretly flicking peas and bread pellets at a young woman who merely laughed?

"Sometimes," Namour told him cheerfully, "they throw apples and oranges!"

Everyone complimented the gardener and the chef on their skill. But who had paid any attention to what he was eating? No one. La Quintinie, at sea among all these people, remembered the slow development of his asparagus, his peas and his figs, the steady circulation of the sap through the branches, the travail of his trees struggling every day against cold or thirst in order to give of their best.

"What about a game of billiards, messieurs?" said the King suddenly, wiping his fingers on a damp napkin. Everyone stood up. Except the gardener. He stayed where he was.

"Are you coming with us, La Quintinie?"

"Yes, Monsieur de Namour, I'll come."

He waited until the last guests had left, then slowly made for the door, which was still wide open. From the Salon de Diane he could hear the courtiers going into ecstasies over the King's dexterity.

Then he went straight on down the corridors, and came out into Le Nôtre's gardens.

The sky was full of stars. From behind the dark façade of the château came the exclamations of thousands of courtiers. The flickering of torches, reflected in the surface of the ornamental ponds, illuminated the other side of the sky. He walked past the orangery towards his moonlit garden. What had he to do, he wondered, with all these people who knew nothing of the world, which they kept at arm's length with layers of powder, high heels, wigs, jellies and sauces? All these people whom he had just watched devouring in minutes what had cost him a lifetime to produce. All these people who trifled with too rich and too abundant a supply of food, and who gradually forgot what they were themselves.

"How right you were, Philippe, when you said we forgot everything and forgot ourselves all the time. As Ecclesiastes says, 'All the labour of man is for his mouth, and yet the appetite is not filled.' The little church in the village of Versailles is soon to be demolished. And do you know what Mansart is going to build on the site? The servants' quarters.

"But you still haven't answered me, Philippe. Where are you? Do write to me."

→>-<←

Weeks went by. The King hadn't been unduly surprised or annoyed by his gardener's disappearance. It was well-known that he was a strange, unpredictable character. But he had no equal in providing for the King's table. And was not the Grand Dauphin about to become a father? This news, which would put an end to the rumours circulating about Monsieur and his friend the Chevalier de Lorraine, occupied all the time and all the thoughts of the King, who had perhaps never been in such good humour.

→>-<←

Every morning the gardener vanished, and he didn't come back before nightfall. His assistants were worried to see their master abandon them, just issuing a few half-hearted orders before going off.

"What can have got into Jean-Baptiste to make him behave like this?"

"How should I know? Ask him."

"And have him tell me to mind my own business? No thank you!"

"So what can we do?"

"I don't know."

"Perhaps he's in love!" someone suggested, making everyone laugh.

"Why not? It would explain a lot."

When for once La Quintinie stayed in the garden, his staff would watch him surreptitiously while he earthed up his artichokes, bound his lettuces, trained the runners of his strawberries, pinched out superfluous shoots. And they smiled at the thought of this little man buried in the skirts of a big fat woman.

La Quintinie spent most of his days at the nearby farms. It was to these poor people and to them alone that he gave all his time and all his knowledge. In return, having nothing, they gave him what is beyond price: themselves.

The peasants' harvest promised to be especially good that year.

➤◄

He found the letter pushed under his door when he came home late one night from seeing the Berniers.

"Monsieur La Quintinie —

We do not know one another. My name is Jean Migault and I come from Mougon. Monsieur de Neuville has spoken to me about you often, very often. I wanted to write to you before. Monsieur de Neuville died two weeks ago, at our house, fortified by the last sacraments. Forgive my clumsiness — I don't know how to put all this. He had been slightly wounded by a shot from an arquebus a few days before the dragoons left. Perhaps he wrote and told you about it. But despite the care he received the wound never closed. His blood became tainted, and although he was bled his condition grew worse. Before long he was unable to write or speak. For a time we hoped he would get better. He has been laid to rest in the graveyard in Mougon. Do you know if he has any family? We would be happy to know you, Monsieur de La Quintinie, because you were his friend, so if you came here —"

The letter fell from the gardener's hands. His eyes seemed to rove vainly round the great void created by the news he had just read. Nothing was left around him but the silence of the night. A deep, dark night that gradually engulfed him completely.

→>-<←

He rose hours before dawn. He walked. Above him the sky was lightening in a wide, pale blue, almost white gash. The wind stole over the crests of the hills, between the tree trunks, under the sparse vault of their foliage, spreading scents of sap and dead grass.

At a turn in the path La Quintinie stopped by the shattered façade of a deserted farmhouse. He could see into the ground-floor rooms. He went up a narrow staircase to a partially collapsed first floor, then climbed higher to even dimmer recesses. The house was almost entirely covered with ivy, its gnarled branches stifling the memory of all the men and beasts who once lived there.

The gardener walked on.

By the time he reached the Berniers' cottage the last stars were vanishing from the far side of the world.

XXI

One morning from the direction of the château a column of black smoke could be seen rising slowly into the air, which suddenly began to echo with sounds of shouting and frantically pealing bells.

"Fire! Fire! The château is on fire!"

The wind changed, burying the garden in a cloud of acrid smoke. Everyone rushed to the scene, dropping whatever tools he'd been using and snatching up a bucket, a blanket or a spade. Without stopping to think, La Quintinie joined in with the rest.

But when they reached the Place Royale the gardeners met with an unexpected sight. Hundreds of men and women were singing and shouting and dancing around a gigantic brazier, while others were feeding the flames with anything they could lay hands on – cranes, scaffolding, sedan chairs, scraps of panelling, pieces of parquet.

But what was going on? An uprising? Perhaps. There were many workmen among the crowd. But no – there were a lot of courtiers there too.

One of them noticed the gardeners standing there dumbstruck, not knowing what to do with the implements they were carrying. He hurried over to them.

"Today's a great day," he cried, his eyes bright with enthusiasm. "Come and join in the dancing! Look!" – he suddenly pointed to the right — "There they all are!"

"But what is it? What's happening?"

But the man was already making off, and his answer was lost in the clamour that rose and fell like a wave in time with the flames.

Groups of peasants now started to emerge through a thick curtain of smoke, drawing along behind them cartloads of marrows, asparagus, peas and apples. La Quintinie immediately recognised the fruit and vegetables he had so painstakingly helped his neighbours to produce. He hurried to meet them.

"What are you doing here?" he asked them. "And why all this fruit and these vegetables?"

Their faces lit up with broad smiles.

"Oh, Monsieur de La Quintinie — you're here too! We heard the news!"

"News? What news?"

"Don't you know? Canto and his criers came to tell us — Madame la Dauphine gave birth to a son this morning!"

"What about it?"

"What do you mean, what about it? It's wonderful news!"

"But . . . What are these carts here for?"

"Presents for the Grand Dauphin, the Dauphine and their son! We don't have much, as you know better than anyone. Just some fruit and vegetables. But we hope the King and Monsieur his brother will deign to accept our gifts. We owe so much to you, Monsieur de La Quintinie. Now, please forgive us, but . . . you understand . . . you see . . . we'd like to . . ."

All eyes turned towards the bonfire. All ears heard only the cries of the crowd. The gardener moved away.

As the peasants passed him he recognised the faces and voices of the men he had thought he knew so well and for whom he had done so much. He stood without moving, waiting for them to go by. Drawn by the light of the huge bonfire, they had all come to dance beneath the balcony of a King who had better things to do than bother about them, though life had made them pay so dear for what they had come to offer him.

→>-<←

La Quintinie went back to his apartments. Alone. His assistants had left him to join the others in the marble courtyard.

In his room he remained standing despite the fits of dizziness assailing him. In the distance he could hear the cries of people full of excitement about an event that had nothing to do with them. From further away still a rumble of thunder came from between the clouds. It was going to rain.

The tenuous link still binding him to the world of men had suddenly snapped. And now he was far away, sinking swiftly and soundlessly into the void he had never been able to fill.

He had a vision of Halley's comet. Why hadn't he understood its meaning before, why hadn't he realised that sign from heaven was meant for him? Why hadn't he seen that all this life, his life, had never been anything but futility and lies? Titles and fame were lies. It was futile to think oneself free, different from others, protected from the disasters of the world by barriers of walls and leaves. Futile to think one controlled the universe when it was the universe that governed us. Nothing but pride to believe that one might some day turn the world upside down and change the people who lived in it.

He thought of Neuville and Dancourt, buried beneath earth that was not their own; of their vain attempts to escape the toils in which fate had held them, like everyone else.

He thought of the courtiers and their King, of men and the

societies they construct but which wear out, disintegrate and are forgotten, then rise again from their own ruins.

He read again the verses from Ecclesiastes that he had copied into his journal: "I made me gardens and orchards, and I planted trees in them of all kinds of fruits: I made me pools of water, to water therewith the wood that bringeth forth trees ... Then I looked on all the works that my hands had wrought, and on the labour that I had laboured to do: and, behold, all was vanity and vexation of spirit, and there was no profit under the sun."

XXII

 The gardener had disappeared again. But no one who worked in the garden was worried: he was probably with his precious peasants. Besides, winter would soon be here and there was much be done. Potting, earthing up young trees, spreading straw on the artichokes, gathering crops, planting, sowing, preparing storerooms.

More days went by. And eventually people started to worry about not seeing La Quintinie when they arrived in the early morning or left late in the evening after putting their tools away. There was still no light to be seen in his apartments.

When they told the King of their fears he was incredulous.

"Come, come, messieurs — you know him as well as I do!"

When they persisted, guards and pages were sent to see the peasants and make inquiries there. But the gardener seemed to have vanished into thin air.

➤►◄◄

When Louis, one of La Quintinie's workmen, arrived at the staff entrance to the garden that morning he found some of his colleagues gathered there in a state of unusual agitation.

"But I've seen him, I tell you!" Charles was protesting, waving his arms in his excitement. "He's in the old strawberry greenhouse at the end of the garden."

"What do you mean, 'in' it?"

"This morning I came a bit earlier than usual to see to the parsnips. With all the rain we've been having these last few days, I was afraid —"

"Yes, yes. So?"

"Well, just as I was going to collect my tools I saw him in the distance coming out of the strawberry house with a watering can. He filled it at the big ornamental pool, and then he went back into the greenhouse."

"And then what?"

"That's all."

"What do you mean, that's all?"

"Well, that's all. He didn't come out again."

"Didn't you go and see what he was doing in there?"

"No."

"Perhaps instead of just talking about it we could go and find out what he's doing," Louis suggested.

They all went and gathered quietly around the greenhouse, which was still shrouded in early-morning dusk. Charles was right: a faint light could be seen gleaming fitfully through the dusty window-panes. They made out a shape moving to and fro inside.

"Is it him?"

"Yes."

"What shall we do?"

No one had anything to suggest. They stood there for some time watching the little light, which from time to time was obscured by the indistinct shadow of their master. Then the candle went out and they went back to their work. But all that day they couldn't help glancing towards the greenhouse in which their eccentric master was now confined.

The days never seemed long to him in there. He had marked out some beds, broken up the soil and sowed seeds. Very soon, encouraged by the gentle warmth that came through the window-panes, the first shoots had burst through. He stood there now, upright in the middle of a world of stems, stalks and burgeoning leaves. And it seemed to him he was growing and developing at the same time as his plants.

+>-<+

Sometimes the whole place was pelted with deafening deluges of rain. The gardener disliked such days on his own account, but he welcomed them for his plants. The time went by peacefully, measured out by the sound of drops beating on the glass. He waited for the end of such dull days gloomily enough but without impatience. Memories would arise in his mind's eye: of the dry land of Italy, dotted with cypresses; of the trees of his child-hood; of the lofty skies of the Charentes, his home, skies so lofty and wide that he'd known that for him life could never consist in anything else but belonging to the earth, where death and the sap of life flow together in a single stream.

+>-<+

The greenhouse slowly filled up with leaves and flowers and with insects he no longer drove away. It filled him with wonder to lift up a tuft of grass and find underneath it a whole seething nation of legs and feelers, horns and scales. Some plants were dying from the attacks of weevils, mole-crickets and earwigs, and this was a spectacle that always saddened him. But he liked to think that one death meant another life. Everything in existence was a matter of exchange and self-giving. The insects bringing death to the plants would die in their turn, offering up their pale bellies

[113]

to other roots, which would thence derive the energy to thrust a new stem up into the light.

Absorbed in the silent adventure of nature, the gardener eventually forgot the clocks and calendars of the men he sometimes heard passing nearby – men whom he in his twilit greenhouse no longer wanted to know, and who gradually receded from his sight, blotted out by layers of foliage.

How many years, how many lives would it take him to forget completely what he had learned so quickly out in the world of men?

→>-<+

The King himself took the trouble to come, accompanied by some of his courtiers. He ordered a servant to knock at the door, call La Quintinie by name. In vain. He soon realised he had put himself in an undignified position: what was he, the King, doing there, standing helplessly outside a silent closed-up greenhouse? He turned on his heel and left.

"So what's to be done, Your Majesty?"

"Pooh! Nothing. He's not doing anyone any harm."

→>-<+

As the days went by the assistants got used to living with the mere silhouette of their master, whom they glimpsed from time to time drawing water from the pond, picking some fruit or digging up a few vegetables. At first they tried to make out what his reasons might be for acting in this way, but their questions all remained unanswered and in the end they gave up. Still, they all liked to see the little candle being lit at nightfall, a small light that bore witness, as in the distant dark of churches, to a presence now gone from their midst.

A few days ago winter had descended on the garden with frost and icy winds, sombre skies and pouring rain. In spite of the fire that he kept going all the time, in spite of blankets and layers of clothes, the gardener was shivering. The cold seeped in through every crevice — under the door, around the window frames, through the tunnels made by insects. He had a bad cough. But what was he doing here, in this hostile universe, hemmed in between inert rows of branches? Out there beyond the window-panes were his apartments, a warm room, soft carpets, a comfortable bed. Hot and varied meals, clean water, wine.

Suddenly he stood up, went over to the door, reached out for the door-handle ... Half a dozen times he did this, and half a dozen times he drew back and returned to where he was standing before. Then he took the heaviest things he could find — his desk and his chair — and piled them against the door, wedging them in place with two large water tanks. At last he sat down, exhausted, covered in sweat, coughing. He waited for his heart to slow down, then rolled himself up in his rough blankets and fell into a heavy sleep.

→>—<←

A ray of sunshine pierced the clouds, made its way through a grimy window-pane and alighted on the stalk of a plant. The gardener leaned towards the frail stem, suffering in order to become what it must.

→>—<←

He was waiting. The world was wrapped in a silence broken only by his fits of coughing, each more wrenching than the last. They gripped his lungs in a vice, burned his chest and left him crouching exhausted on the side of a bed dark with earth and sweat.

He staggered to his feet, tottered over to one of the tanks and dipped his hand in the water. Everything was mixed up in his memory. He recognised Philippe's face. Dancourt appeared at a turn in a corridor. Lully and his baton moved soundlessly. Trees and mountains of cloud merged into darkness. His mouth filled with the taste of fruit and of earth. He could hear voices: "Your secret, Monsieur de La Quintinie – don't forget your little secret."

Voices and images alike faded. He sat there helpless, his mind a blank. Then he was seized with a long and painful fit of coughing, more violent than any before. His handkerchief was stained with blood. He suddenly felt the ground give way beneath him. Outside were warmth, food, carpets, paintings, fountains ... His hand clutched at the edge of the tank, he reeled over to his bed, then lay down and waited. His chest felt easier. He could breathe again. The crisis was over.

→>·<←

What day was it? What month? And that bell in the distance – was it for vespers or high mass? He smiled at such trivial concerns. What was the time of men? Days, dates, bearings from which to calculate the distance we have travelled since we were born and the distance we have yet to travel before we die. And those two years, those derisory figures carved on graves, confining each individual for ever within a time, an age ... He thought of the mayflies fluttering around his candle: for them a day was eternity. He thought of the insects' eggs tucked away between two stones, which would one day each produce a larva, a caterpillar or a cockchafer, one of the creatures that would inhabit the world for a few days or weeks and then die without leaving any trace or date. And he thought of the time of men, of its apparent length, of the duration of their empires and of their systems — these too revolved around a distant star, and would soon be burned up before plunging into a vast and ageless night.

In his greenhouse time no longer existed. He was a hundred thousand years old. He had just been born.

+>-<+

The body lay face down on the ground. The ants were the first to get at it, then weevils, aphids, beetles, moths and maggots joined in the feast. They swarmed through the orifices by the thousand; descended into the dark channels of the arteries; they hollowed out new passages in the entrails, slashed at the skin with horns and claws. The gardener's flesh crawled with countless lives.

The earth opened up to receive the bloated, seething corpse, which sank slowly down among roots and bulbs and insects.

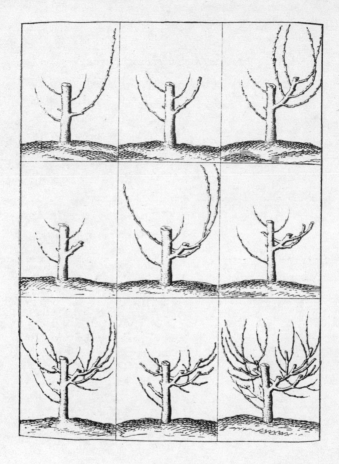